A DASHIE DISCOVERY

A MOBILE GROOMER MYSTERY, BOOK 1

M. ALFANO

Proofreader: Jasmine Bryner
Editor: Helen Page
Cover Designer: Molly Burton with CoverWorks

Whiskered Mysteries
PO Box 1485
Summerville, SC 29484

Dedicated to my husband.
Thank you for FINALLY reading one of my
books and saying "Hey, your stuff is
actually good."

ABOUT THIS BOOK

Hi, I'm Leslie Winters, and when I left Houston for my hometown of Pecan, Texas, I needed a do-over in a big way. So I set up shop in my dad's old shed and took on clients less likely to run off with now-cheating exes.

My pet-grooming business turned out to be a pretty fun way to make ends meet… until I dropped off two tough Pomeranian clients at their home, and found their dead owner waiting for us.

Then local law enforcement finds me at the scene, and my dachshund finds the murder weapon right in front of them. Oh, boy!

Now I'm out to solve the crime before a certain dreamy detective tries to collar me for the crime.

But someone is on my tail, and they're making it clear they don't want me to investigate.

After a few close shaves, I'm now more determined than ever to solve this case. Can I figure out whodunnit before I wind up in deep do-do or worse?

1
_____

Miss Paisley and Daisy Williams clawed their way onto my table.

Stubborn as mules in quicksand, these two ladies got more attention around town than all my other clients put together.

You'd think two little five-pound Pomeranians would be easy to handle, especially when most of their weight consisted of light brown poufy hair. But you would be wrong. Nevertheless, their humans paid me a pretty penny to get them fluffed out in the trademark Lion trim Pomeranian owners loved, even when the Texas humidity wasn't cooperating with their double coats of fur and neither were the dogs.

"Paisley," I whined, at my wit's end. "If you

would just sit still, this would all be over soon, Hun," I chided, trying to push back my bangs. A fight with the water hose and a fidgety Jack Russell had matted my black fringe to my forehead.

Maybe I shouldn't have cut my bangs, and maybe I needed a better set-up than my dad's old shop he used to fiddle around with his tools. But now was my dog grooming shed. Since that would happen anytime soon. I had to work with what I got.

The little tan ball of fur looked up at me from the metal table, her beady little black eyes practically staring into my soul. I bought the metal table at a pawn shop closer up the way toward Crab Apple Canyon. If I went east, toward Dallas, it would probably cost twice as much.

But the old catering cart from a flea market worked when I couldn't pay more than ten dollars for the piece.

The only thing scarier than fear of tetanus from a used table or a Pomeranian's yip would be the scowl from her mama, Mrs. Tiffany Williams, if I didn't have her puppies ready before she headed to the church for the ladies Bunco night.

Every Wednesday, like clockwork, the women of a certain age in my town of Pecan, Texas, on the west outskirts of Dallas toward Oklahoma, got together at the church hall for the dice game and potluck.

I kept one hand on the dog, so she wouldn't leap from the table, sighing to the heavens at my luck to have these two firecrackers needing my expertise at the last minute. Fumbling toward the wall rack, I dug into my secret stash. Usually only for emergency cases, but if I didn't get these girls done and groomed soon, it might be an emergency.

As soon as I had the can of Cheez Whiz in my hand, Paisley finally dropped her rear onto the table, her tongue wagging as she stared at the little white container, ready for me to draw a line of yellow cheese on the table for her to lap up.

"That's better," I cooed, trailing the stream of cheese in front of her nose. Paisley snorted, then dropped her snout to the curled yellow cheese, darting her tongue out and lapping it up.

Primping and puffing Pomeranians while bribing them with cheese wasn't exactly where I saw myself in my early thirties.

But a divorce and moving back to small-town Texas was never on the agenda either.

I'd been a hairdresser in Houston. A mildly successful one.

Ignore the bangs, a desperate post-divorce decision. Along with the hips from a lot of mom's home cooking.

The last few years in Houston, I got by simply fine while I tried to ignore my husband's wandering eye. But when a client showed up pregnant, saying Archie was the dad, I knew it was time to pack up my blow dryer and head home.

Pecan, Texas, set in the shadow of Crab Apple Canyon, population three thousand, already swarmed to Mrs. Bev's hairdressing salon. I wasn't about to compete with the preacher's wife for customers. Though, if I was her, I might have switched up the same gray pixie cut and dark-rimmed glasses made popular by Vidal Sassoon and Mia Farrow in the sixties, but that wasn't my business.

And since I couldn't compete with Mrs. Rosemary's Baby, I figured grooming dogs really wasn't all that different from blowing out Texas beauty queens. Still the same amount of claw marks and a lot of yapping.

The shop I set up was basically a sink and worktable in my dad's garage that he reluctantly let me use, with only a few gripes. Not that the man had actually touched any of the tools gathering dust there for years. He was about three years away from retiring from desk jockeying at the chip factory. He didn't do much when he got off work other than whittling on the front porch or falling asleep to late-night talk shows.

So, Dad had no use for the shop now covered in dog fur. Paisley and Daisy were some of the worst shedding offenders, but the Williams were my best clients, and I wasn't going to turn down business over a small mountain of dog hair. Especially if it would get me out of my parents' house sooner rather than later.

Ma waddled into my workspace from the back porch. "How were the girls today, Les?"

She didn't get out much since Texas summers lasted until October, and she preferred the air conditioning 24/7. But if she was coming down from her recliner perch near the back screen door, then something was up.

She stood in the doorway of the shop, the light glow of the afternoon sun streaming in behind her.

"They were...well...they were them," I yelled over the yapping of the freshly-shorn and sham-pooed Poms as I tried to secure a sequin bow to Paisley's head. I'd given the difficult duo a little trim around the ears, as they say.

I kept my eyes on the little dogs, with only the occasional glance at my mom. The little girls would take the first chance they got to bolt.

Usually, Bandit, my-rescued, ten-pound, chocolate-brown dachshund, the only thing I got in the divorce aside from my ancient SUV, was there to keep watch by the back door of the shop, but he was out sniffing for food as usual. Spring was prime crawfish season, and there wasn't a hole that he didn't love to dig in and chow down.

He'd probably need another bath as well once I got the girls delivered to their mama.

I made the mistake of glancing up as I sat Miss Paisley back down on the table.

Ma fiddled with her ever-present turquoise cross necklace, usually securely pressed into the fabric of her floral house dress.

Who the heck wore floral and polyester in this heat?

Former Miss Pecan, Anna May Winters, that's who.   Her-colored-every-six-weeks-on-the-dot blonde curls sitting in a frizzy halo around her head, only tamped down by enough hair spray to leave a giant hole in the ozone over our heads.

I quickly looked down at my own outfit.

Leggings and a t-shirt, both covered in dog hair.

My stick-straight black hair in a messy bun. If Ma wanted to argue about what I was wearing while leaving the house, as she often did, I was going to have to make a quick exit.

"Ma, is everything okay?" I didn't really want to know the answer, but I was a polite southerner, after all.

She twirled that necklace around a full turn before she finally tossed her arms out. "Okay, fine, Leslie, it's too hot out here to beat around the bush."

She paused long enough to pull a battery-operated fan from her fanny pack and blow it against her face. "Archie called the house again."

Even in the heat, my ex's name could bring a cold chill down my spine, shocking me like an early frost. "What did he want? He has my cell phone number."

Not that I would have picked up while I was working. Or anytime for that matter.

"Heavens, I don't know, Leslie. He was jabbering on about being sorry and begged me to have him call ya." She shook her head, the whirring of the fan buzzing between us.

Ma clucked her tongue. "I bet his mama's been bothering him again. That woman always thought she was God's right-hand woman, sitting in the front row at church every Sunday, looking down on everyone she passed in her giant Suburban. Now she's got a divorced son and a soon-to-be grand-baby out of wedlock. Ain't that some karma?"

Ma didn't need to remind me.

Mrs. Blank and I never saw eye-to-eye as it was. She never thought anyone was good enough for her Archie, even his high school sweetheart, who didn't do a darn thing but support him through real estate school and numerous moves all over Texas.

Now every time she saw me in town, she was just as sweet as a Fredericksburg Peach. Probably hoping I didn't tell the town gossip mill about her golden child.

She was just lucky one of us knew how to keep our mouth shut.

"I have to deliver the dogs to the Williams' ranch. If Archie calls again, just let it go to voice-mail or something."

I finally got Daisy into her little pink harness just in time for the Poms to start their yapping again.

"You're gonna have to talk to Archie someday, you know," Ma called over the dogs.

"Maybe someday I will, but first I gotta get

these dogs home before Bunco," I yelled, grabbing the dogs' fancy leather leashes complete with gold trim. The things had to cost more than my own purse and were way too nice to use as doggie accessories.

"We'll be home soon, girls. Don't worry," I cooed as Ma put her hands on her hips.

"I swear, Leslie, if I didn't know any better, I'd say you're ignoring not only Archie but me as well."

Well, duh.

But I wasn't going to tell her that.

My parents had been nice enough to take me back in. Even with the gossip mill of a one-stoplight town.

As soon as I got on my feet again and maybe found a nice salon that I could rent a chair from, in the suburbs and the housing market was reasonable enough to find a house or cheap apartment with a low pet fee, I'd be out.

That's what I'd been saying the past six months, too. Packing my spare tips away in a sock drawer and the rest of my money going toward pet grooming supplies.

I was the only game in town for now, but surely there would be someone else coming up behind me soon.

But I didn't plan on staying back in Pecan forever.

As if Bandit knew I needed him, his little heels scraped against the wooden porch and made his way past Ma's legs and into the little shop. The scent of pond water and sunshine greeting my nostrils before he poked his little furry head up.

"Bandit, my stars. Again?" Ma called.

Paisley and Daisy started up their barking again as they spotted the little-silver clawed creature dangling out of Bandit's mouth.

"Girls, quiet. It's just a crawdad," I yelled, trying to balance the dogs on my hip, their leashes flying around as they tried to squirm out of my grip.

Bandit rounded Ma's heels as she fluttered her hands, screaming like a banshee which did nothing to calm the dogs squirming against my chest.

The leashes went flying as two balls of fur flew out of my arms, running after the little lobster trying to make its way to the closest water source it could find.

It didn't get too far before Bandit had it back in his mouth, tossing it in the air then back on the ground.

Paisley and Daisy did an excited yip, and before

I could stop them, both girls decided to roll in the now-deceased little crustacean on the floor.

"Girls! No! No!" I picked them both up as quickly as I could, both of them now fidgeting wildly in my arms. Which of course, did nothing to help the scent of fish now wafting off their just groomed bodies.

"Good heavens, Bandit," Ma called, putting her hand to her chest and looking down at my dog, who snorted before rolling over the dead little mudbug himself, an almost smile on his snout.

"Well, I guess I'd better give these girls another rinse," I muttered.

"You'd better. I don't know why he insists on bringing those things around all the time. Do you think other dogs do that?" Ma asked.

I shrugged, putting the dogs back in the big tub that Daddy usually used for cleaning up after working on the lawn, but I had now repurposed as my dog bather.

Ma huffed. "Okay, well, as long as you're good in here, I'll head inside."

Bandit hopped up to his back legs, whining up at Ma.

"Oh, fine." She gave him a little scratch behind

the ears. "You're lucky you're cute, even if you do get into everything."

He snorted in response.

Which is what I wish I could have done too.

But now I had to rinse the dogs and get them ready again. If I were even a minute late, who knew where my already tarnished reputation in Pecan would be because of my little Dashie's discoveries.

2

___

Bandit rode shotgun, his ears blowing in the breeze of the air conditioner. He'd been my constant companion since I first saw his picture posted on the Crab Apple Canyon Shelter Facebook page. The runt of a litter abandoned near the railroad tracks, Dashi was no bigger than a can of pinto beans in the photo. Families looking for a pet had snapped up his better-looking brothers and sisters, leaving him as the lone pup staring at the camera with those big, beady black eyes and floppy brown ears.

My ex, Archie, didn't want a dog. He had just graduated from the real estate program at the community college, and I was working at a small salon inside Walmart. We'd been married only a few months and living in a beat-up studio apartment on the sketchy side of Crab Apple Canyon. When Archie got home from passing his real estate exam and said he found a job in an office in San Antonio, I agreed to move. On one condition: we adopt the little puppy at the shelter.

Now, years later, it was just me and my trouble-making dog. He may have been still awake in the front seat, feeling the breeze through his ears, but the two little Pomeranians snored in the backseat.

Guess the second bath had knocked them right out and good timing before we drove through downtown Pecan.

If one could even call it that.

My parents' house was at one end of the Pecan grove, the town's namesake that lined a small walking trail and the sidewalk up to the courthouse. Each tree followed a cobblestone path past the post office, two Mexican restaurants, and a couple of little shops that seemed to rotate as boutiques or resale shops every few months.

Since it was a historic main street, at least the exterior of everything looked great, with the same wrought iron awnings and pillars lining each little storefront. No matter what was inside. This month we had a new antique store, aka grandma's junk shop, in place of a former baby boutique and a furniture restorer replacing a gluten-free bakery. That place only lasted about a month in town before they chose not to renew their lease, and the owners headed back to Dallas.

But the town still had something incredibly charming about it that had people coming back and settling in the shadow of Crab Apple Canyon.

Past the small town square, Pecan Baptist, the first of one of the three Baptist churches in town, and even farther past the only bar in town, The Boot and Saddle, you'd finally come to the Williams Ranch.

The grand stucco Mediterranean-style estate lay just outside of town in an unincorporated area on a few thousand acres.

Rumor had it around town the former Mrs. Denise Williams hated the sprawling seven-thousand-square-foot house. Something about it being too big and too much to clean, even though we all know she had a housekeeper who did everything.

So, when Mr. Williams hired a new assistant to help with the house, Mrs. Tiffany, and she started spending more time at the ranch, it ultimately led to the former Mrs. Williams' demise: A broken heart.

That and fifty-plus years of smoking unfiltered

Pall Malls and living on a diet of Diet Dr Pepper and deer jerky.

But I wasn't one to judge anyone's habits, especially those of a woman's past. I was just there to see the new Mrs. Williams and to get a paycheck after dropping off the snoring bundles of fur in my backseat.

Pulling up past the long white horse fence, I made my way to the wrought iron gate and arch engraved with Williams Ranch hanging over me.

I made sure not to push my car ahead too quickly and hit the gate as I entered the key code.

Slowly, the large fence swooshed open, leading down the long cement path into the portico of the large brick and flagstone structure.

Bandit whined from the front seat, staring at the longhorns in the pasture like they were expecting him to come graze in the field with them.

"Now, boy, I can't have you going out and rooting around. Who knows what you'd bring up to the doorstep? The crawdads are big enough in our back pasture. Imagine how big those things would be from all the fertilizer in the yard?"

He let out a snort as if he were resigned and then curled up on the seat, his head on the console as he let out a big yawn.

"Yeah, guess you had a rough day, too?"

I ruffled his ears one last time before letting out a breath.

Opening the back door of my old SUV, the two dogs stirred from their slumber, all of a sudden wide awake and sniffing the air as if the smell of cows and grass were welcoming them home.

Carefully I unbuckled them from the back, one at a time, smoothing down their coats and adjusting their little satin bows one last time before leashing them up and heading to the double front doors.

"You stay here, Bandit. I'll be right back," I called over my shoulder as he stared at me from the open passenger window.

After rounding the display of cacti in the big red rocks, I stepped on the front porch and rang the doorbell, but it was almost just a courtesy since Paisley and Daisy were already pawing and barking at the big metal front doors. No matter how big that house was, someone had to hear them.

Yet, I heard no movement behind the large glass panes, so I rang again, tapping my foot as I counted backward from ten.

Mr. Williams' truck was parked in the circle drive, just south of the giant cement fountain, complete with dancing longhorns and water shooting out of their horns. I figured Tiffany's Mustang was in one of the six-car garages.

Yet, no answer.

This time I put my fist to the door, the metal bolts clanging against the white stucco of the house as I knocked harder.

Slowly the door creaked open, not shut all the way.

Well, this was Pecan. No one locked their doors, so I guess this could be expected.

But I wasn't about to just let the dogs loose and have them pee on one of the Persian rugs in the grand foyer.

Using one hand as I entered, I tried to shut the door behind me, but it was enough of a lead on Paisley's leash that she sprang out from my grasp, her little claws clacking on the marble floor as she ran full speed ahead, past the foyer and the stained glass windows and into the living room.

Deer and goat heads lined each wall, flanking a large stone fireplace and a room full of dark leather furniture. Every surface was covered in something cowhide or bearing the Texas star.

"Paisley!" I hiss-whispered, trying to catch up to her with Daisy pulling me along.

Dang, they were strong for such little things.

If there was an intruder, we'd definitely given our location away.

My shoulders relaxed when Paisley scratched at the sliding glass door, and I saw the back of Mr. Williams' Stetson hat poking out of the hot tub.

The Williams' pool looked like something straight out of a design magazine with its limestone fountain and grotto.

The hot tub, though, was a favorite place of Mr. Williams. He liked to soak with a good cigar after work while a brisket smoked on the nearby outdoor kitchen barbecue.

Everyone knew Mr. Williams liked to bathe in one of those embarrassing tiny European suits some men wore, so I always tried to avoid their backyard when he was there.

Now where the heck was Mrs. Williams?

Both dogs headed straight for the hot tub, yipping and pawing at the water.

"Great," I muttered under my breath.

Guess Mrs. Williams wasn't coming out, and I'd have to scrub my eyes later.

I opened the door, the Texas sunshine already beating down on my neck. "Sorry about that, Mr. Williams…"

Rounding the corner of the grotto, I made my way to the tiki bar.

As my eyes adjusted to the afternoon sun, I finally saw Mr. Williams. All of him.

Face down in the water, wearing nothing but that Stetson hat and tiny pair of swim trunks.

"Mr. Williams?" I went to poke his body but didn't see any movement. His pruned body, bobbing against the jets.

I grabbed my cell phone, dialing in 911 as fast as my shaky hands could move. I guess things weren't so quiet in Pecan, Texas, after all.

3

———

Bears have four paws, five toes and long, sharp claws.

I know this because I've been looking at this giant Bear rug, complete with a head snarling at me for the past hour.

I've tried not to look at anything but this stuffed bear head while EMTs and Pecan's police force have swarmed the scene as I sat shivering on the buttery leather couch.

Last time I saw this many first responders was at the annual Fourth of July barbecue at Pecan Baptist. But this was a far cry from the long line for Pastor Dave's pulled pork tacos.

Luckily, one of the local boys recognized Bandit

pawing at my car window and brought him inside to me.

My little Dashie immediately curled up on my lap, placing his head right underneath my neck and tucked in for a snuggle.

Running my fingers up and down the coarse hair of his back was always a good coping mechanism when I had to deal with any kind of stress. Whether it was a bad client. Bad divorce. Or, you know, walking in on one of my clients who just met their maker.

"Hey, how are you holding up?" The sugary sweet voice of Mr. Williams' only daughter, Haley, was the only thing that tore my gaze away from the bear's glassy-eyed stare.

She was a few years younger than me, but I vaguely remembered the bookworm when she was a freshman and I was a senior. Pecan High was small enough that everyone knew everybody else even if we ran in different circles.

Not much had changed in the fifteen years since I'd graduated and last saw Haley. Same frizzy brown hair and thick glasses, but at least she'd lost the braces.

Though they were hard to see since her lips were turned down in a frown, her hand on my shoulder as if I were the one that needed to be comforted.

Wasn't my dad in the jacuzzi.

I turned, taking both of her slender hands in mine. "Oh, don't worry about me, Haley, how are you?"

She was always a small girl and looked even more so in the large sweatshirt that seemed to swallow her whole five-foot frame.

Wasn't it a little hot for an A&M hoodie?

April in Texas was always unpredictable but golly, in this heat?

And wearing that school of all schools embroidered across her chest.

Her dad would probably be rolling in his grave if he saw that since he'd always rooted for the Longhorns.

As did most men in town. Couldn't go anywhere without someone yelling, 'Hook 'em, horns!

Though not many men had actually left the town to go to college there, it was still a sense of pride to cheer for University of Texas in Austin, no matter what.

"I…" Haley shook her head, closing her mouth then opening it again.

Before she could respond her head whipped toward the front door where a flurry of blonde curls and southern sass ripped through like the tornado belle she was.

"Y'all. Oh my god!" Tiffany Williams heels clicked on the floor as she ran inside, her face covered in mascara-streaked tears.

"Jesus, she's here," Haley muttered under her breath, not looking up at her stepmother, who happened to only be fifteen years older than Haley herself.

Tiffany sped past the officers, stopping just a few feet in front of me, the scent of her floral perfume and Mrs. Bev's casserole wafting off of her curvy body clad in way-too-tight-for-church-jeans and an off the shoulder top that put her bronzed shoulders, and other assets in the low-cut neckline, on display.

"Leslie, I got here as fast as I could. I went to the church early to help set up for Bunco and…"

Tiffany put a manicured hand to her face and looked over at her stepdaughter. Not a single wrinkle or line on her face. Botox so she didn't move a muscle or was she just that good at piling on the makeup?

"Oh, Haley. Hun, have you seen him?"

Haley didn't respond as we sat there in an

awkward silence that luckily only lasted a few seconds before Deputy Grant sauntered over.

He'd been one of two cops in Pecan for the last ten years. I'd only had a few run-ins with the curly-haired, mustached officer, his love for donuts evident in the pants he never seemed to be able to button, a large paunch, and a Texas state belt buckle.

Mainly Deputy Grant and I crossed swords when he flagged me for driving too fast down Main street. But late, our interactions involved just a quick 'hello' when I dropped off his wife's prized poodle, Lilly, at their home after grooming.

This time he wasn't smiling or holding one of his favorite donuts.

His blue uniform wasn't even starched, and I'm quite sure he missed a few buttons in his rush to throw it on.

Definitely out of his element. This was the biggest thing to happen in Pecan since a few kids pulled a senior prank and stole the fire truck, going for a joy ride for a few blocks before Deputy Grant caught them and their mamas gave them holy heck.

In all my years in Pecan, there had never been anything like this.

"What in the heck is going on in here?" A bristled voice called, bolting through the door.

Everyone's gaze turned toward Edgar Williams, Mr. Williams' brother in all his larger than life glory.

Not that either of the Williams boys were small men, but Edgar had a voice that carried through a room, sometimes with bits of spittle or whatever his wife, Mrs. Susan, the elementary school music teacher, cooked for him.

"Edgar," Tiffany turned, her hand still on her chest, ever the southern belle.

I couldn't help but notice his eyes wandering toward his late brother's wife's chest, but he quickly composed himself, running his fingers through his whitening stubble of a beard and down the bolo tie pressed against his starched yellow button down.

"Listening in on the police scanner, I heard there was a commotion, so hopped on the four-wheeler and came right over."

"It's Billy…he's…he's…" She couldn't finish her sentence before the water works started and Edgar, all too eagerly I might add, held his arms out, letting her collapse in his big open arms.

"Mr. Williams." Deputy Grant cleared his throat, rounding out our little circle.

Edgar looked over his shoulder, his big blue eyes widening. "Is it…is my brother okay?"

There was emotion to his voice yes, but something was lacking. Something that had me thinking there was much more to this cozy little set up with Edgar and Tiffany.

If my mother knew I was thinking those thoughts, she'd send me right to the church.

But I was quite sure something was off about the whole meeting.

Something that screamed, "THIS SHOULD BE INVESTIGATED."

I had to get out of there. Away from this whole scene. Too many late-night mystery podcasts had my mind going into overdrive with theories and possible suspects.

"You know, if it's all right with y'all, the dogs are here, and Bandit is probably ready to eat something, so I'm just going to head out…"

Slowly, I rose from the sofa, setting Bandit down on the floor next to me. He snorted like I was the rude one to wake him from his slumber but he happily trotted along next to me.

Though we didn't make it more than a few paces before running into a firm wall.

No.

Not a wall.

I looked up to meet a pair of dark eyes narrowed right at me.

Jumping back, I straightened out my shoulders, meeting the gaze of a man in a black suit with a full head of wavy brown hair, and at least a day's worth of stubble.

Stubble on a pair of dimples.

Wait, who was this guy?

And why had I never seen him around Pecan?

Dang it, Leslie, stop checking out random hot men.

Hiding my heated face, I looked down at Bandit, who didn't have the decency to be a guard dog and bark at the man. Instead, he just sniffed around his shined loafers, wandering toward the front steps like he was hot on the trail of something.

Possibly a bug.

Or Tiffany's bluebonnets.

"Nobody is leaving right now, not until I ask a few questions," the man's deep voice crooned, forcing my head to snap in his direction.

I put my hands on my hips.

Just because he was pretty didn't mean he was going to give orders.

"I have to get my dog home, Mr. Suit Man, and

I don't know you from Adam, so if you'll please just step aside."

Those dark eyes were back on me, a slight smirk crossing his face. "Ma'am, I'm Detective Adam Waltz from Dallas Homicide, and this is an active crime scene, so you will do what I say."

Homicide?

Dallas?

In our town?

Swallowing hard, I tried to look anywhere but at his steely glare and that was when I spotted the bushes moving.

No. Not the bushes.

"Bandit!"

My yell was enough to distract the detective as I rounded the other door and grabbed my little Dashie by his collar, pulling him out of Mrs. Tiffany's prized marigolds.

But it wasn't a mouth full of yellow flowers that he unearthed.

"Step back, ma'am." Detective Waltz was at my side, holding out a plastic baggy as he called for a pair of men in latex gloves.

The world moved in slow motion as from my dog's jaws they pried a pearl handle, attached to a rusted out antique pistol.

"This belong to anyone before I take it into evidence?" Detective Waltz asked as he held up the bag, the gun now waving like a white flag.

Glancing behind me, the crowd from inside now gathered on the front porch, but none of them could look at the detective.

Even Edgar, who usually had a comment for everything, shifted from one foot to the other, his mouth shut.

Something told me that there was more to the story of poor Mr. Williams' death, and whatever it was, it wasn't going to be figured out by a big city detective.

This was a job for a Pecan girl.

4

"I told you the story one-hundred times now, I don't know what more there is to say."

Detective Waltz, or should I call him Adam? sat across from me at the oak dining table, clicking his pen as he stared over the wrought iron centerpiece.

He had one of those hard expressions that all the *bad cops* did on late night reruns of court shows.

If he thought that would work on me, then he'd never seen my mama's face after breaking curfew as a teen. She would cut her eyes at me, and I'd just know to shut my mouth.

Bandit escorted back to the car by one of the local officers after being dusted off after finding an antique weapon, the local boys now fawned over him, probably giving spoiling him with more treats than necessary.

"Yes, Mrs. Blank, but…"

I held my hand up, cutting him off.

At least the man had the good sense to close his lips and stop talking.

"It's Miss Winters, but as I've already said, please, call me Leslie."

He peered down at the sheets in front of him. "Is there a reason for the different name on your driver's license?"

I threw my hands up. It took everything I had not to roll my eyes. Lord, if my mama knew my thoughts right now.

"Are we here to talk about me and my name change because of my divorce or the guy in the hot tub?"

Waltz nodded, scribbling something in his notebook, his lips in a thin line, not giving away a blink of his thoughts.

"What's that? What are you writing? Are you trying to say now that somehow I'm the one who…"

The end of the sentence fell before it reached the end of my tongue.

I still couldn't say it.

Sure, the obvious conclusion was out there in the open with a gun found in the bushes and the very dead man who had been wheeled off to the morgue.

But Mr. Williams was dead.

Someone wanted him that way.

And every time I thought about seeing him bobbing in the water, a ring of bile rose in my throat that I had to quickly swallow down.

Detective Waltz looked up from the other end of the table, still no change in his expression. Still the bad cop.

"Like I said, Leslie, just asking some questions since you were the one to find Mr. Williams, and your dog found that piece of evidence outside."

I blinked hard. "The piece of evidence? That gun is a historic .38,\ Smith and Wesson, complete with wooden handle. Not in particularly good condition, albeit, but who knows if that thing can even shoot? Might have been there for years."

His pen scribbled across the paper, but those dark eyes trailed down the length of my dog hair-covered t-shirt.

Sure, I had some curves, not all in the right places with Ma's home cooking every night, but was this man seriously checking me out right now?

No…

He was seizing me up.

Did he think I was the killer?

If I were, I'd definitely do a better job hiding the gun than having my dog bring it out.

Wait, what was I saying?

I couldn't think like a killer.

I shook my head, swallowing down whatever thoughts kept popping into my brain.

"Huh."

"Huh what?" I asked, turning my attention to him.

"Interesting you know so much about weapons."

I rolled my eyes, this time not able to hold it back. "Growing up in Texas with a daddy who hunts, it isn't hard."

"Fair enough."

He scribbled down some more notes then shoved a blank piece of paper toward me.

"I'm going to need your information, you know, in case we have any follow up questions."

I raised an eyebrow, trying to ignore the little prickle on my skin from his earlier ogling. "Like you want my number?"

He smirked. "Your full name and number for the investigation, Leslie."

"Oh, yeah, right."

Heat flushed my cheeks as I put my head down, hoping he didn't see the little embarrassment ruffling my feathers. I wrote down my contact information, sliding the paper back across the table before glancing around the room.

Haley was sitting on the leather sofa, her uncle perched on the arm of the chair next her as he patted the back of her arm, whispering something I couldn't hear.

Tiffany sat at the breakfast bar, talking to a couple of uniform officers, her dogs propped up on each arm.

I had absolutely no business being here when a family was grieving and yet, something still gnawed at the back of my brain.

So many questions that the detective probably had ready to check out, but no one did sleuthing like a woman in a small town.

"Is it okay if I head out? My dog probably needs some water, and I've got to get home."

Detective Waltz nodded, clearing his throat as he stood up with me.

The man had to be at least a foot taller than me

and the scent of coffee and leather seemed to waft off him like a tidal wave.

"If that's all your information, then of course, I'll walk you out."

It was only a few steps from the dining room to the front door, but with every movement my heart thumped faster.

Who had just taken these last steps before I came in?

Who had it in for Mr. Williams?

The Detective let out a breath as if he were going to say something, but before he could, the front door cracked open.

I couldn't see who was behind it, but by Edgar's standing bolt upright, waving his gums a mile a minute, I only had one guess.

"Susan, where in the heck have you been? I was calling and calling."

The door shut behind Mrs. Williams in all her five-foot-music-teacher-soprano-voice-glory. She was wearing her trademark floral muumuu and brightly colored blazer with stiff shoulder pads. Her bottled red hair fell in soft curls down to her shoulders, matching the coke bottle red glasses perched on her nose.

Susan and Edgar had been married for as long

as I can remember, back when he still had hair, a waist, and everyone thought he'd be running the ranch.

Hmmm…that sounds like a motive for killing your brother.

Wait. No. He wouldn't do that…would he?

"I was getting my hair done. You know the color has to set. What's the big fuss about anyway and why all the brass?" She fluffed her hair off her shoulders, peering around the room.

"I think that's my cue…"

I slowly slunk around the door, leaving the couple and detective to go over what happened.

Bandit eagerly waited, panting with his little furry head hanging out the window, acting like he was the most pathetic dog in the world, even though I saw little bits of donut crumbs still on his snout.

"Sorry about that, boy," I cooed and got into the driver's seat, trying to block a barrage of pawing as I reached into my glove compartment, pulling out a stash of Sonic napkins and a pen I got from the bank.

Placing one of the wrinkly brown squares on the steering wheel I smoothed it out and started my list.

Possible suspects

1. *Brother*

Well…it was a start at least.

What I needed was someone else to help me with this.

Someone I could trust, who watched more true crime than anyone I knew, and by the way my stomach was rumbling. I knew just the lady to head to.

I just hoped the bakery was still open.

5

"Bubba, if you don't leave your sister alone, I'm gonna get the spoon."

The six-foot-tall woman stood on her front porch, dark blonde ponytail covered in flour all the way down her oversized white t-shirt and black leggings. The screen door behind her still open and wafting out the most delicious smells in three counties.

I was lucky that Sophia and I had been friends since grade school, and she was the best home cook in town.

Her son let go of his sister's hair, a gummy smile crossing his toddler face as soon as Bandit jumped out of the car.

"Is this a bad time?" I asked, careful not to step

on any of the dozens of hot wheels cars littering the yard.

Sophia waved her arm. "Come on, just getting a set of cookies out of the oven for an order. You can watch me make the icing."

Score.

My mouth watered before I even saw her delicacy of butter and whipping cream.

"Bandit, you watch them." She pointed a finger at my dog, happily on his back, getting pets from the two young kids.

"Are they okay out here?" I asked tentatively, looking from the happily prancing Bandit to the kids, sans shoes, playing in the dead grass in desperate need of treatment as the watery days of April would soon bring the heat of the Texas summer.

Mind you, I didn't have kids of my own but wasn't sure the protocol of having them play in the front yard.

"Randi knows not to go in the street and they'll be back inside in two seconds anyway," Sophia called over her shoulder. She'd almost reached the kitchen as I trailed behind.

Sophia and her middle school principal husband, Jake, lived in a house with a white picket fence complete with shutters and a big front porch on a quiet cul-de-sac. Well, was quiet probably until they moved in, and their kids started running around.

I always admired how they had their lives together and furniture that didn't come from an online shopping discount site.

Everything was always spotless, looking like an ad in a pricy catalog with their leather couches and coffee tables not chewed up by a dog.

Footsteps creaked on the wood floors as the screen door shut again behind us, followed by a round of giggles.

"Told ya," Sophia called over her shoulder before turning into her kitchen.

When they bought the house, Jake agreed it was time for Sophia to finally get her dream kitchen. But not long after closing, they found out they were pregnant with baby number one and maybe buying a crib was more important than a Subzero fridge.

So, after each tireless wedding and birthday season, they'd replace pieces of the green and yellow linoleum kitchen. Though now it was a hodge-podge of various kitchen gadgets and an array of mixing bowls and cookie cutters mixed with kids coloring crayons all along the butcher block island.

"So, not that I don't enjoy your company, but did you come because you heard about my cookie order for Mila Garcia's Quinceanera, or do you have something else on your mind?"

Sophia barely looked up from the red mixer, placed a little too close to the edge for my liking.

I glanced behind me, making sure the kids were occupied before I leaned in.

"I just got done with taking the girls back to the Williams' ranch."

She huffed. "What the heck did Tiffany do now? Another boob job? Spend Haley's inheritance on some new lawn art? That fountain is one of the most awful things I've ever seen. Did you know they paid someone eighteen-grand for that custom piece? Eighteen-grand! And that doesn't include installation."

I bit my lip, fidgeting from one foot to the other as I tried to come up with my response. "Well, I'm not sure Tiffany's done anything."

Her eyebrows rose, and I sucked in a deep breath.

"I found Mr. Williams…"

She covered her mouth. "Oh my gosh, did you see him naked? Gross, gross, gross."

Well…he wasn't totally naked.

I closed my eyes, shaking my head before opening them. "He was murdered."

Sophia dropped the spoon in her bowl, her mouth hanging open. "You've got to be kidding me."

I quickly went through the less gory details, including the arrival of the detective and Dashi finding the antique gun in the hedges.

Sophia listened intently, not saying a peep and nodding, her spoon and frosting long forgotten.

"So…what happens now?" she asked.

"Well, the detective took my number for any follow up…but…"

"But?"

"I don't think some guy from Dallas knows any more than us."

She blinked hard before a smile bloomed across her face. She clapped her hands, and did a little hop that was probably a little too giddy for what I was suggesting. "So, we're going to do our own investigating? Like we've planned to do in a podcast for years? Who else knows more about late night crime shows than us?"

"The podcast? Really? I thought that was always a joke after how much we binge watched." It took everything I had not to roll my eyes.

"Yeah, but we're both really good at it. You always know who did the crime whenever we watch those late night shows on ION." She beamed.

"I mean…as long as we don't hurt anything or get in the way of the police, I don't see why not. Heck, we'll probably have it figured out before them, and they'll give us a medal or something."

"I like the way you think. Now, help me finish up this frosting so we can get to work before Jake gets home."

I nodded sagely, knowing her level-headed husband wouldn't approve.

But it was for the good of everyone that Sophia and I figure it out.

And if I could get some of her leftover frosting and cookies while we did some internet sleuthing, then all the better.

6

With the cookies chilling, the kids entertained with an iPad, Bandit snoring on the couch next to them, Sophia and I set to work before Jake got home.

She booted up her laptop as I took a seat next to her at the breakfast bar, pushing some random decorating supplies aside.

"Okay, first up, the Pecan Neighbor app," she said typing in the address.

"Isn't that where people post things for sale and missing dogs?" I raised an eyebrow.

She nodded, not looking up from the screen. "Uh huh. They also post questions when something is up. Like someone shooting off fireworks at two in the morning or a missing package. These people on here are some of the nosiest and best detectives around, so surely someone had to post something we can use."

I nodded, mulling over what she said. "Okay, maybe you're right. What are people saying?"

"I'm getting there, I'm getting there."

Sophia scrolled through posts with various baby clothes for sale and people looking for lost goats. Then in between an ad for a lady's makeup business and a missing dog, we struck gold.

Subject: What's going on at the Williams ranch?

"Bingo," Sophia whispered, opening up the convo.

BevJohnson: "I was on my way to Bunco when I heard the sirens heading down FM 6. A bunch of em. Hope the Williams are all right."

RobbyWood: No smoke or ambulance at the ranch from what I can see from the shop.

. . .

LouiseJones: @TiffanyWilliams
Anything you can tell us?

I leaned in as if somehow the answer would magically appear on the screen, or at least Tiffany would reply.

Instead, just more skepticism.
Maybe it was another big delivery for Tiffany, Ha ha.

Probably just another brush fire. People gotta stop with that burning their trash when there's a burn order.

No one can take anyone's freedom away. Let them burn and order what they want!

. . .

"Well, that was a dead end," Sophia grumbled. "But we still have Facebook."

"Ugh…can you really trust anything people put on there? Ma shared an article with me from the other day about a theory that a former missing kid from the seventies is now a White House reporter. And she took it as gospel from one article from a source that also shares ads for fat burning tea."

Sophia shook her head, her fingers tap, tapping along the keys. "Yeah, everyone shares everything on Facebook or more like overshares."

She scrolled down the screen where a few people had already posted rants about their kids' teachers or passive-aggressive-remarks about neighbors being too loud on a week night.

Then in the middle of all the crazy, Sophia stopped scrolling, the words practically glowing on the screen.

Piper Mason: Prayers for the Williams family

"What does she know?" I whispered.

Piper went to school with us, and besides being

the captain of the cheer squad and having the biggest hair, she had a reputation for still knowing everyone's secrets.

The garage door echoed, shaking the jars of spices on the wall.

"Dang it, what's Jake doing home?" Sophia slammed her laptop shut right before Jake walked in. As soon as the hulking six-foot-five-inch balding man, clad in gym shorts and a polo shirt, came through the door, he was immediately taken down by yelling kids practically pulling his britches down his skinny legs.

"Hey, Babe, hey Leslie," he yelled over the kids screams and made sure his drawers didn't drop.

His eyes were slightly narrowed as he ran his hand over his bristle of blond hair, looking between the two of us. "Staying out of trouble."

"Always." Sophia put her hand on the counter as she shot me a conspiratorial glance.

"I should be heading home. Ma's probably wondering where I am."

Before I could get Bandit away from licking a few bits of caked-on peanut butter from the cabinet, Sophia called over my shoulder.

"So, I'll pick you up for Awana's tomorrow?"

"Um, what?" I turned slowly, trying to read her expression.

Awana's had been around as long as the town of Pecan itself, where parents could drop their kids off for discipleship and a free dinner

She lowered her chin, jutting it out at the same time. "You know, the kids' program at the church. Piper Mason asked us to help out?"

Ohhhhh.

Okay, so this was where the investigation was taking us.

If I'd watched as many late-night crime shows as she did, maybe I'd have a similar idea.

Or caught on quicker.

"Yeah. I'll be ready then."

Coaxing Bandit away from the sticky cabinets, I led him out to the still-humid night air.

As soon as I pulled out of the cul-de-sac, I let out the breath I didn't know I was holding.

"Well, Bandit, what do we think?"

He kept his little bobble head on the window, staring out into the fields as we made our way back to my parents' house.

The Texas star solar lights Ma had hung on the front porch were just starting to flicker and sway. Not dark enough for a full glow and the breeze probably more likely from pushy swarms of mosquitos than any weather.

Ma and Pops had lived in the little ranch style house on an acre lot since they were first married. That was before people started building on our little street and you could see across the fields, practically all the way to the Dallas skyline on a clear day.

But now everything had built up and the town I never thought I'd live in again was here, welcoming me home.

With a murder.

As we came through the back screen door of the house, Bandit immediately ran for his food bowl, chomping down the kibble. A foil-covered dish sat on the stove top, the smell of chicken fried steak and gravy still wafting in the air.

At least Ma got the Texas home cooking gene.

Me?

I burned macaroni once and figured I'd save everyone the trouble by learning to make a mean charcuterie board and memorizing takeout menus.

But before I could even peel the aluminum foil back, Ma's voice travelled over the TV re-runs blasting from the living room attached to the little galley kitchen.

"Les? Is that you?"

No, it's a robber who would dare go through a gate with a sign hanging off a rusted gun shell reading 'We don't call 911'.

I winced, like a teenager who just got caught sneaking in after curfew. "Yeah, Ma, it's me,"

Though my teenage days were long gone and technically I wasn't hiding anything.

Technically.

She shuffled into the kitchen, already in her robe, her reading glasses perched on her nose as she looked down at me like a child who was about to get reprimanded.

"So, your dad heard some interesting news when he stopped by the Quick Stop on his way home from work."

Here it came.

She put her hands on her hips, taking over the whole doorway and blocking my exit to escape. "When were you going to tell me about what happened at the Williams' ranch? Is it true that ol' Billy was found naked as a jaybird in the Jacuzzi?"

"Well, technically he had on a really small pair of swim shorts and his hat."

"Leslie," Ma bellowed, stomping her foot.

Sighing, I wrapped my dinner back up, knowing the delicious crispy dish was going to have to wait until this conversation was over. "Yes, Ma, I was the one who found the…"

Body didn't seem like the right thing to say.

But, heck, what did you say in this situation?

Instead of bile rising in in my throat this time, something else rose to the surface.

I blinked away the tears threatening to impede my eyes.

Why was I crying?

It's not like Mr. Williams and I were best friends or anything, but this was a life.

A life that was taken.

Ma dropped her hands, tilting her head to the side as her face softened. "Oh honey, are you okay?"

Better than Mr. Williams.

"Yeah, just a lot to take in…"

"Did they find the guy who did it? I bet it was Edgar, not the sharpest tool in the shed, but he always did have a grudge against his brother."

That comment piqued my interest as I wiped my eyes and took in a big sniffle.

I leaned into the old Formica counter that Dad kept promising to replace. "Why do you say that?"

A throat clearing huff came from the doorway, and we both turned to see Dad sauntering toward us. Like Ma, still in his bath robe, but his was more tattered, yet it made the big ol' cowboy with his white handlebar mustache look like the man who used to clean his shotguns on the front porch to intimidate my high school dates when they'd come to pick me up.

"I don't think it's wise to talk about the dead like this, or the living for that matter." He ran his tongue along the front of his teeth, raising his bushy eyebrows as if saying 'y'all understand what I'm saying about the gossip?'

Ma nodded. "You're right, Wendall. Not right to talk ill about the dead."

She may have said the words, but if I knew anything about my mother, as soon as Dad left for work tomorrow, she'd probably have already read every Facebook post and talked to all the church ladies to get the full scoop.

"You good, Les?" Dad asked.

I nodded. "Yeah…I'm good."

Though, was I?

As I ate my dinner in the little dining room, just a few steps from where my parents watched some old sitcom reruns, my mind kept flashing back to poor Mr. Williams.

And to what Ma had said about the brother.

Edgar seemed super distraught when he got to the ranch, but was that all an act?

And what about that rusted gun? Could that really be the murder weapon?

After cleaning up my dishes, I took a quick shower, pulled on my pajamas, and crawled into my old bed.

I recall first night I slept in my old room again at Christmas that still had my old white wicker day bed and matching vanity and dresser. It felt like taking a step back in time. Even when I moved away from home, Ma hadn't changed a thing, right down to the old lacy pink comforter.

But now with Bandit curled up next to my pillow and the scent of lavender and dryer sheets surrounding me, I took in a deep breath for what felt like the first time all day.

Before I could even try and close my eyes, though, the light familiar tapping rapped at my door.

"I'm decent," I yelled.

Slowly the door creaked open, but Mom's head full of fabric curlers soon blocked the sliver of light from the hall.

"Hey, Les," she whispered, closing the door behind her as she padded across the hardwood floor, her furry slippers barely making a sound even with her heavy footfalls.

Well, since I wasn't going to get any sleep, I figured I'd sit up, wiping my eyes to adjust to see better in the dark.

Bandit snorted, curling up closer to my side as I leaned back against the wicker headboard.

Ma edged toward the bed before slowly sitting down, her weight shifting the mattress. Even in the dim light streaming in from the window, I could see her biting her bottom lip, fidgeting with that turquoise cross just like she had earlier when she was telling me about Archie calling.

"Everything okay, Ma?"

I sat up even straighter, wondering where this clandestine conversation was going.

"I don't know. Is it, Les? You came home from seeing a man meet his maker." Mom blinked hard, clasping her cross necklace as if it were a buoy keeping her afloat.

I swallowed hard, the emotions of the day wearing on my already heavily-loaded shoulders. "Honestly, I don't know, Ma. It's crazy. Murder in our small town? That just doesn't happen."

Ma nodded slowly, twisting her necklace the

same way I was guessing the wheels were turning in her head.

"And you said you thought Edgar might have something to do with it. Think that's something we should say to the cops?" I pressed. I hoped this was the case of her nerves. She'd tiptoed into my room because Dad was probably asleep on the recliner, snoring loud enough to wake the neighbors, and she had nothing else to do.

"Oh, honey, that was just me thinking out loud." She waved one of her hands like she was swatting a fly, but the other remained tightly clasped on her cross.

"And you were thinking…?"

She blew out a raspberry. "Oh, fine."

I leaned in closer, Bandit taking that moment to curl on my lap, his big furry head pressed against my stomach.

"Those two boys have been fighting over their parents' property for as long as I can remember. Even when the old Mr. Williams, crotchety old fella, God rest his soul, was still alive."

"Fighting? Like physical? Legal?"

I leaned in closer, straining for every detail.

Ma pursed her lips and nodded. "You name it.

Only reason Billy got the property was because of some money troubles that Edgar got in from what I hear. He and Susan were mighty ticked when that happened a few years ago. After a few glasses of chardonnay at Bunco a few weeks ago, Susan couldn't stop rattling on about how Billy didn't deserve it all because Edgar couldn't handle his money."

I blinked, trying to take in all of this information.

Maybe I needed to go to Bunco and talk to Mrs. Susan, too, after she'd had a few glasses.

Ma patted my knee. "But, honey, this is nothing for you to worry about, okay? That's their family matters, and I'm sure it'll all get figured out. You have enough going on."

She raised her eyebrows as if magically I was going to spill out that I loved Archie and would forgive him and take him back so we could all be back in the good graces of his mama.

"Yeah. I'm really tired, Ma. Maybe we can chat more later." I yawned, stretching my arms over my head for good measure so she'd get the message.

Ma nodded, but that hand kept twisting her cross around her neck. "Okay, honey. I'll see you in the morning."

She got up slowly, her eyes still on the bed as she

backed out of the room, probably praying on that necklace I'd call her back for a heart to heart.

But I had bigger problems than just my ex-husband to think about.

Now with Ma's new info, I had even more puzzles crashing through my brain.

I took in a deep breath, trying to clear my mind.

Then let it out once my phone buzzed with a text from my nightstand.

Sophia: So, you're going with me to Awana's tomorrow, right?

Glancing at the full moon out the window, I thought about how Mrs. Tiffany was looking at that same moon. What was going through her head right now?

And was that handsome Dallas detective already in bed, not giving a lick about this case? Just another note in his book?

Me: Yep. I'll be there.

I put my phone down and curled back under the covers, hoping my dreams weren't filled with visions of dead bodies and irritable Pomeranians.

7

Pecan Baptist Church was a pillar of the community. Along with about five other churches in the same small town, all scattered across Main street and the town square. All vying for the same patrons.

Though Pecan Baptist liked to tout that it was the oldest church, erected sometime before the great tornado of 1920 that destroyed half the town. Though. back then, the teetering brick structure probably stood like a beacon. Now, with all of the metal building add-ons for kids' programs and Women's Bunco, it looked more like a slap-dash warehouse.

One way to guarantee they kept people coming back, though, was to provide free activities for children on a Wednesday night.

Usually, I did everything I could to get out of volunteering to hand out chips to a bunch of screaming kids from preschoolers to sullen high schoolers.

Yet…here I was, standing behind the large Formica counter, wishing I'd brought ear plugs for the sheer amount of shrieking that could come from tween girls.

Sophia smiled, handing a girl with rainbow braces a juice box before she looked at me.

There's something about being friends with someone for so long that you could have an entire conversation with just one flick of your eyebrows.

And Sophia's definitely said, '*I swear this will all be worth it*'.

But after about the fiftieth screaming kid, who supposedly attended an evening event to learn about the bible but swore like a truck driver, I was definitely wondering if I would have been better off at home with my mom's judgey glances and cross twirling.

And if things couldn't be any worse, one of the many volunteers had to be my ex-mother-in-law.

Mrs. Blank was supposedly the head of the church's board, but what she did for them, I had absolutely no idea. Just standing there in her pearls and floral day dress, looking down at people like she did every single Sunday, and now I had to see it on a Wednesday night.

I prayed she didn't notice me behind the counter and cardboard cutout of Mary and Joseph. But of course, I could never be that lucky.

"Leslie, hon, longtime no see." Her sugary voice reached the hairs on the back of my neck. I could feel them standing straight up at attention.

"Hi, Mrs. Blank," I managed to not spit out like venom, but kept my head down, focusing on handing the chips to each freckle-faced kid that came to the counter before they headed to one of the folding tables in the big hall.

"Archie said he's been trying to call ,and you haven't been answering. I didn't think you were too busy, seeing as how there can't be that many dogs in town that need grooming."

She smiled with those way too bright red lips. She'd given me the exact same color of lipstick one Christmas.

I then threw that 'Dragon Girl' color away as soon as I got home and bit my tongue on saying how perfect the name was for my dragon lady of an ex-mother-in-law.

I opened my mouth to speak then closed it again like a floundering fish.

I couldn't say what I really wanted to say to the dragon lady, because we were technically in the house of the Lord.

If you considered the big metal, echoey building attached to the back of the church, the house of the Lord, that is.

But now that she was staring at me with that same judgey look I'd been trying to avoid, absolutely no words were coming out.

"Why don't you go and see if Piper needs any help, and I can hand out the rest of the chips?" Sophia said, way too loudly, getting a few looks from the other tired moms who were looking more at their phones than the snacks they handed out.

Definitely ignoring the one sandwich and one cookie rule per kid. But I guess they weren't their children so no harm for them if they sent them home all sugared up.

And, if she was going to save me from my ex-mother-in-law, I'd take it.

I nodded, knowing I'd have to give her a big thank you later.

"Yeah," I said, taking off the latex gloves,

tossing them in the nearby bin before rounding the counter to the fray that was the large fellowship hall that the church used for everything from funeral pot lucks to vacation bible school.

Just like Sophia predicted, Piper Mason was holding court like only a life-long-Pecan-resident and Pee Wee cheer coach could.

Technically, I wasn't even sure she was volunteering, but at five-foot-nothin', with her hands on her hips, her dark bun giving her another six inches to her height as she loomed over a group of tweens, she even had me standing at attention.

The bright fluorescent lights didn't do any of us any favors and showed every tear and scowl from the sullen kids gathered around the folding tables.

"Okay, y'all, a few more minutes and it's time for gaga ball." She clapped her hands together in quiet, rapid beats, ever the cheerleader.

I had no idea the dress protocol for volunteering, if it was Sunday best, or what, so I wore a sundress and some strappy sandals. Both I quickly regretted once I was tossed an oversized lime green shirt with 'volunteer' vinyled on the back and told to wear it over the dress.

No wonder my ex-mother-in-law was giving me such dirty looks.

Piper, though, was owning that shirt. She looked like an Olympic coach with the bright shirt hugging her small frame and her tights showing off her muscular thighs from years of cheer and coaching.

She worked as a loan officer for the bank now, but she had to be doing something else to get those biceps. Maybe I'd ask her someday…when she didn't intimidate me.

"Hey, Piper. Thought maybe you could use some help." Dang it, why was I so nervous? Piper was only two years older than me, and we weren't in high school anymore where she had been the popular girl, queen bee.

Did one ever grow out of that in a small town?

"Hey, Les, yeah, I could definitely use some help wrangling up the kids."

I glanced at the group of tweens who were already packing up their stuff, throwing away their plates in the big plastic garbage bins, like obedient angels, or ones who didn't want to hear the wrath of the bedazzled whistle dangling from Piper's neck.

"Okay. I think I can handle that."

We walked behind the group of kids out of the church and through the sticky Bermuda grass to the large, wooden octagon used for Gaga ball.

From what I could tell, it was basically like

dodgeball, but in a sand pit with a fence around it that I'm fairly sure the farmers also used for herding goats. I just hoped the foam ball the kids were throwing at each other wasn't as hard as the rubber balls of dodgeball I remembered from my youth. I could deal with attitudes, but blood? Nope.

And at a church camp?

I guess things were different from the fire and brimstone preachers of the day.

So now what did I talk to Piper about?

Did I ask rules about Gaga? Maybe that was a good segue.

Looking at our feet instead of trying to figure out how she got those strong of calf muscles, I noticed her shoes. The bright teal color that could probably glow in the dark.

"Hey, nice shoes. I think I saw Tiffany Williams with a similar pair, are they comfortable?"

Piper stopped just outside the court, lifting up one foot than the other. "Yeah, we both got these at the outlet in Grapevine. Buy one, get one deal. Can't beat that."

"I didn't know y'all were shopping buddies." I leaned in closer, hoping I didn't come off too eager.

If I did, Piper didn't seem to notice. "Well, I was up there with Gabby, getting new shoes for camp and ran into Tiffany. We both needed new shoes, and it ended up working out great for all of us. She even got a pair for Billy, bless her heart."

Bingo.

I sighed, trying to add in an extra breath to really lay it on. "It's awful what happened."

"I heard you were the one who found him," she said, her tone not sharp exactly, but tinged with speculation.

Okay, if I wanted the goods from her, I could give a little.

And this was better than being inside and having to dodge questions from dragon lady while handing out chips.

I nodded. "Yeah, was delivering the dogs, then as soon as I went onto the back and saw him, I called the cops."

"So, you did see him? My sister heard he was shot, square in the forehead."

How did this lady and her sister get so much information so quick?

I gulped. "Well…he had on his hat so I didn't see much…"

Piper put her hand on my shoulder, squeezing what I'm sure she thought was gently, but pinched a little too tight for my liking. "Bless your heart, that had to be awful."

"Yeah. Poor Tiffany was distraught."

Piper nodded, putting her hand down. "Yeah, one of the off-duty officers came by Bunco to tell her, and immediately she was crying. She had to sit down in the sanctuary for a while before she could even drive home."

I shook my head. "Awful. I don't know who would do something like that to the Williams' family."

She snorted, but then quickly covered her mouth, shaking her head. "Sorry, I shouldn't laugh."

"So why the laugh then?" I raised an eyebrow, my heart beating just a little bit faster as I leaned in to hear.

"Billy and Tiffany had more enemies than a bear in a beehive. Surely you knew that?"

I blinked hard. How long had I been gone? I thought everyone was fond of the Williams' family. Well except the old Mrs. Williams, rest in peace.

"Really?"

She glanced at the kids, who paid no mind to us, so deep in their game, yelling 'Ga' and throwing the foam ball. Her voice lowered slightly as she looked down at her shoes, tracing a line in the dirt.

"I don't want to speak ill of the dead, or my friends for that matter, but I know a lot of the ladies at church weren't too pleased about Billy and Tiffany in talks to sell some of their ranch land."

"Selling?"

So, Ma was right about the feuds with money. Mrs. Susan probably had a lot to say if they were selling the land and making money for it when she thought that money and land should go to her and Edgar.

Piper put a finger to her lips, glancing over her shoulder. "Tiffany said they'd been getting offers in from land developers, wanting to add more neighborhoods and even a Wal-Mart. I wouldn't mind not having to drive half an hour to get my groceries, but some of these ladies aren't too keen on new developments coming out this way."

Especially a drinking Mrs. Susan.

"Keen enough to do something about it?"

Piper lifted her hands. "I'm not saying that. I'm just saying, there were plenty of people riled up about that one."

I didn't even have a second to think about which

ladies were at Bunco that night before my name came out in a quick bark.

"Miss Winter."

My spine straightened as I turned to see Detective Waltz in the light glow of the church lights just starting to turn on as the sun set.

He was in another similar button-down shirt as the first time I saw him, though this time the sleeves rolled up, his tie gone, and the collar popped open. His hair looked rumpled as if he'd been running his fingers through it all day, trying to figure out how in the heck a small-town rancher would end up dead in the hot tub.

Annnnd probably came to the same conclusion I had about investigating at Awana's.

"Can I have a word with you." It wasn't a question; it was a command boring from those deep brown eyes.

"Do you know this man?" Piper whispered, her eyes wide and the wheels already turning, trying to figure out how she was going to find out the latest gossip probably.

"Detective Adam, didn't expect you to be an Awana's man, but if you want to go see Mrs. Bev inside, she'll get you a volunteer shirt."

"Miss Winters." This time his words were crisp. To the point. His eyes narrowed.

"Okay, okay, I'm coming." I looked back at Piper, her eyes searching between the detective and me. I swore smoke coming out of her ears as the wheels turned. "I'll be right back, okay? Just holler if you need me."

She nodded, then I followed Detective Waltz to the edge of the parking lot, trailing behind him like a little kid walking the green mile to the principal's office.

He leaned against the dark SUV, crossing his arms over his chest in a stance that was probably supposed to show his power, which he did a fairly good job of since the man had better biceps than Piper.

Not that I was checking him out or anything.

"What is this I hear about a young brunette going around town and asking questions on social media?"

"Young brunette? Well, I don't know about the young part. And this isn't brown. This is ebony black, thank you."

He sighed, pinching the bridge of his nose. "Miss Winters, this is an ongoing criminal investigation. This isn't some Nancy Drew game of Clue."

"Those are two completely different things."

"Miss Winters," he barked.

"I told you, Detective Waltz, it's Leslie."

He sighed again, tilting his head back. "Leslie, you can't go around sleuthing an ongoing criminal case."

I scoffed. "I'm not sleuthing. You make it sound like I'm walking around with a magnifying glass, looking under rocks."

"Seeing your name pop up over and over on internet discussion boards is pretty much the same thing in this day and age."

The tips of my ears burned. "So, what if I am asking questions? I found a dead man when I went to drop off his dogs. Don't you think I have a right to know what happened?"

He shoulders finally relaxed as he nodded. "Everyone will what happened in good time, Leslie. But you have to let me do my job, okay? There could be someone extremely dangerous out there, and you wouldn't want to cross paths with that person."

I blinked, a lead ball sinking in my gut. "I didn't think of it that way…"

He closed the distance between us as I sucked in

a deep breath, inhaling his manly scent of leather and coffee.

"I promise you, I'm doing everything in my power to bring this killer to justice. If you need it, I can have a patrol car sent to your place."

Was that...concern in his voice?

I swallowed hard. "No, I'm fine. Really."

"So, does that mean you're going to stop this little Nancy Drew act?" He raised his eyebrows.

"I mean...I was thinking more Olivia Benson from Law and Order..."

"Leslie..."

I sighed. "Fine. I promise."

"Good, thank you."

Out of the corner of my eye, I spotted a familiar glaring face in the window of the "house of the Lord."

Mrs. Blank was probably texting her son right now that Leslie was outside talking to a handsome man in a suit.

Good, let her think whatever she wanted and report back to her son.

I had other things on my mind.

Like maybe a little sleuthing I promised not to do, but nothing wrong if I had my fingers crossed behind my back.

Yes, it may have been dangerous and there was still that sinking feeling in my gut.

But it wasn't going away until someone got to the bottom of this.

And I just had to hope the detective, or my ex-mother in law for that matter, weren't the type to deliver a covered dish to a grieving widow.

8

I wasn't exactly the domestic type. Never got my mom's cooking genes or figured out Mee-maws famous gravy recipe. My former mother-in-law would always make an off the cuff comment on that when she'd visit, we'd head to a restaurant instead of me cooking.

But she wasn't my mother-in-law anymore, and I didn't exactly have the extra funds to pick up an order of tamales.

I figured the church ladies had the casserole brigade covered at the Williams' place to feed Tiffany and Haley for a few years.

So, wine and dog treats were just as good of a covered dish as anything, and no one complained if the peanut butter apple muffins were a little burnt.

Surely the little dogs didn't notice even if they were supposed to start out as people muffins.

Maybe I should have asked Sophia for a batch of cookies, but she was elbow deep in a baby shower order. If Jake knew what we were doing, he'd probably shoot the idea down quicker than my muffins hit the top of Ma's oven.

One that I promised I'd clean up when I got home via a sticky note affixed to the counter next to the stove.

I left Bandit home for this excursion, something he pouted about until I stuffed a Kong with peanut butter.

I couldn't have him distracting me, though he'd been a surprisingly good detective finding the gun, maybe the actions of the two other dogs in the house might help me find something else.

Dogs are intuitive like that.

If something is out of the ordinary, they'll be the first to yip and not leave it alone until someone resolves it.

And if I knew anything about Daisy and Paisley Williams, I knew those dogs would be anything but relaxed.

When I pulled up to the ranch, even through the thick foliage of blooming magnolias I could spot Tiffany's bleached blonde blow out on the porch.

She sat, swinging on the giant wooden plank rocker, complete with a Texas star headrest. A hot pink Yeti clasped in her hand as she waved her other perfectly manicured fingers.

Forcing a smile, I scooted out of my SUV, juggling the bottle of wine and box of "muffins" in the other hand.

"Hey, hon, do you need some help?"

She may have asked the question, but her rear didn't move from her rocker.

The scent of fruity sangria drifted over her perfume as soon as I passed the agave plants and made it onto the sprawling front porch.

Someone already started happy hour.

I guess it was better than having beer bottles splayed all over the place like some sort of fraternity house.

Not like they had any neighbors who would complain.

From the top of the hill, I could see acres and acres of rolling fields with a few cattle grazing.

There wasn't a piece of grass out of place in the yard nor a flower in the garden bed or any of the heavy wood chairs on the wide porch.

"I should be asking you the same thing. How are you doing?" I asked carefully, looking from her cup to the corkscrew she procured from the cup holder in her rocker, already peeling back the wrapper on the wine bottle as soon as it was out of my hands.

"I mean, as good as one can be, huh? Drinking on my front porch on a Thursday night? Want a cup?" she asked, already adding the white wine to her Yeti in big sloshes.

Hopefully, that didn't fall and stain that pretty painted concrete.

Paisley and Daisy pawed at the front door, and I turned toward their little yaps. Both had their heads poking between the wrought iron bars of the double doors, their tails wagging, no doubt hoping I'd come to bring them something. Nice way to break the tension, girls.

And maybe to come out and help with a little investigation.

Lord, if my mother knew I was thinking about interrogating a widow about her murdered husband, she would have had me right to church.

"I also brought the dogs some treats, Tiffany." I held up the small white box, the burnt little loafs looking a bit more appetizing when out of the open light.

"Leslie, you're always so thoughtful. Everyone else has been showing up here with their casseroles, hoping to get the latest gossip on what's happening, but you, you're genuine."

Her cold, clammy hand grasped mine and I tried not to flinch, instead forcing a smile.

"Do you want me to, um, let the dogs out? Or does Haley have them?" I asked, the paws scratching against the posts like nails on a chalkboard.

Tiffany blew out a raspberry "Pft, Haley. She hasn't been back since...well...you know..."

Her slurring words had now turned into a blubber as she sniffled then took a big gulp from her Yeti.

She leaned back in the rocker, letting the wood frame clank against the stucco of the house behind her. Did she notice she'd barely missed the big picture window that looked onto the formal dining room?

One I didn't know if they ever used. A shame with the big clawfoot table and chairs that Mama said were custom-ordered from a place in Oklahoma.

Though I wasn't having any dinner parties either.

"Oh…" It was all that would come out of my mouth as I looked at the floor instead of Mrs. Tiffany.

I wasn't the best with dealing with emotional people.

Or people in general if you asked my ex-husband.

Thus, why we had no dinner parties at the old Houston apartment. Or was it because of my husband's wandering eye? Take your pick.

But I had a good ear for listening and could do one heck of a blow out, so it always worked in the hair dressing world.

Though now my ears were tuned to Tiffany's words about Haley being gone ,and I was going to focus on that instead of rehashing on my own past.

Where did Haley go?

As far as I knew she still lived at the ranch now that she was done with school and looking for a full-time job. Guess, like hairdressers, it was hard to become another accountant in a small town.

At least that's what Billy and Tiffany said the little bookworm was majoring in.

I made a mental note to get to talk more to the youngest Williams.

"When Edgar came over the other day, talking about selling the property, Haley stormed off, muttering about her daddy not even being in the ground and Edgar's trying to roll him into his grave."

I blinked, trying to let the words hit my brain before I spoke.

"Edgar wants to sell the property. Like the ranch?"

Could he even do that?

She snorted. "I'm surprised someone hasn't written that on Facebook or somewhere already. That man and his wife might be family, but they've been trying to get Billy to sell the ranch off to developers ever since I've been with him."

So what Piper was saying was starting to make sense. If Edgar and Susan were being this pushy...?

Motive?

I swallowed hard trying to keep my thoughts tamped down instead of blurting them out.

"I'm sorry he's doing that, Tiffany. I really am." It was all I could say, though my wheels were turning.

If I were a detective, or at least Nancy Drew, what would I ask next?

What had I learned all those nights watching *Murder She Wrote* with Mee-maw?

"It's all right. Once we get to the will reading, Edgar won't have a darn thing to say. It's all written out plainly in black and white."

"What is?" I leaned forward a bit, resting my hip on one of the porch rails, trying not to appear too eager, but my heart was racing.

"Why the property, of course. After Bonnie died, and we got married, Billy wanted to do some reconfiguring, so the ranch and all the assets were put into a trust."

"So…what does that mean?"

Maybe I should have Googled all of this type of jargon before I got there. But now, with my pounding heart, I was all in for her answer.

"What it means is, even if Edgar and Susan wanted the land, they can't get it since they aren't beneficiaries of the trust. That belongs to Haley and me. And neither one of us are wanting to sell so they can put up a dang Wal-Mart or a subdivision in our backyard."

There was a lot of 'we' going on, but I still didn't know what Haley really thought of this.

And if she was as innocent as she made herself out to be.

Though if what Tiffany was saying was true, Edgar had a lot he'd want out of his brother in selling the land.

Maybe even enough to try and intimidate him with a gun?

My racing heart now thudded hard in my chest.

How close had I been to a murder and murderer?

"Well, good for you for standing your ground."

"Thank you. I'm glad you said that, because you wouldn't believe how many people are trying to say otherwise. Honestly, I'm dealing with my husband, my stepdaughter who won't answer my calls, and all of this with the ranch. It's like, what's next? Is Edgar going to drive his golf cart over here and pee in my magnolias?"

I blinked hard, shaking every other thought out of my head. "Has he done that before?"

She rolled her eyes. "Anything is possible on golf night. I swear, him and Billy would say they were playing twilight golf, but when they didn't roll in until one in the morning, smelling like whiskey and cigars, I knew they weren't really doing anything more than hanging at the club house after maybe a hole or two."

I was all too familiar with the Pecan men's way of playing golf. Archie always made his "deals" on the golf course. Which meant a lot of time on the drink cart and I'm fairly sure his custom clubs that I got him as an anniversary gift had cobwebs.

But what else were these men doing on the golf course?

And after a few drinks would Edgar be as forth-coming as his grieving sister-in-law?

9

My southern manners said I had to stay and make small talk with the widow, chugging wine from her Yeti, but my mind was elsewhere.

"You know me and Billy…people didn't agree with our relationship…"

Uh huh.

I nodded, trying to keep my focus on the conversation at hand. Even though it went in a million different directions with each new sentence.

Sip.

"The church almost didn't want to marry us, but I think he might have given Pastor Dave a half a steer. He says he didn't, but that man was eating like a king for months."

More sipping on her Yeti.

More nodding from me.

When my phone began vibrated in my pocket I silently cheered hallelujah.

Saved by the bell.

Finally, I could excuse myself as she went on a ramble about meat prices.

Quickly, I retried the device, my mom's name flashing across the screen as I let out a deep sigh of relief that I tried to hide from the woman in front of me.

"One minute, Tiffany," I said as politely as I could. "It's my ma, I've got to take this." With that, I interrupted her spew of the latest church gossip, none of which had anything to do with the dirt I'd come here to learn.

Though it was interesting to hear that Mrs. Bev had a temper when it came to Bunco.

Did she have a motive for killing Billy?

Wait, no, she was at the shop that day. Susan was there getting her hair done.

Okay, alibis for both.

Dang it.

Onto the next item of business.

The phone call from Mom.

I slid slowly away from Tiffany, leaning against

the porch just a few steps away. "Hey, Ma, what's up?"

Far enough away from that Tiff she couldn't hear the conversation, I hoped, and close enough I could get hints if her ramblings meant something.

Mom squeaked like a cartoon mouse in my ear. "Leslie, I hadn't heard from you and just saw the mess in the kitchen. Were you cooking? Is everything all right? Is this another one of those spells?"

By "spells" she meant that sometimes when I was overly stressed as a teen, I tried baking.

Nothing ever produced more than a lot of batteries going through the fire alarm. So much so that Dad still raised an eyebrow whenever I turned on a burner.

"No, Ma, was just dropping off a dish to Mrs. Tiffany." I smiled politely at the woman as I said her name, but she was busy with the bottom of her Yeti.

"Oh, dear, hasn't that poor woman been through enough and now you need to subject her to your cooking? Why didn't you get some baked goods from Sophia or ask me to make a casserole?"

"Ma..." I started but had no idea how to finish it.

She didn't need to know I was doing a little

investigating of my own and didn't want to have to explain it to her or that I was fairly sure Jake was home, since Sophia wasn't answering her texts.

I was on my own and, well, I guess my baking showed that.

Something gnawed at the pit of my stomach that I'd been trying to tamp down since Archie and I split.

I had my parents and my friends, but there was something else missing when everyone had their own families.

But I mentally shook those thoughts out of my head. Focusing on this investigation was definitely a way to keep the loneliness at bay.

"I'll be home in a bit, okay? Do you need anything?" I asked quickly.

"Oh, actually, yes. Can you stop by the Dollar General and pick up some dish detergent? We're almost out."

I let out a breath I didn't know I was holding in. Another save by Ma and an excuse to leave Tiffany's.

"Yeah, I can do that. I'll see you soon, Ma. Bye."

Once I hung up the phone, I turned to face Tiffany, her eyes glazing over as she rocked slowly.

What was going on in that pretty blonde head of hers?

Surely, she couldn't have done anything to Billy...

Or could she?

I wondered what that will had to say, aside from her and Haley getting the ranch.

Maybe that's why she left?

There was a scuffle?

Dang it, where was Sophia when I needed her?

I held my breath, letting it out slowly.

I had to leave all these questions for another time. I had somewhere else to be before I could muddle over everything else going on in my head.

"Hey...I hate to leave but my Ma wants me to pick up some dish detergent at the DG. Do you need anything from there? I can drop it off later or tomorrow?"

Tiffany waved her hand. "Don't worry about me, none. I'll be fine."

Somehow, I doubted that even though she gave me a weak smile.

This was the face of someone grieving.

I was very aware of what that looked like.

And now I was quite sure that's exactly the same face I made, staring blankly at the southern sky for weeks after I found out about Archie's cheating.

Though this was different.

There was a very dead husband that Tiffany was going to bury in the ground.

And I wasn't going to figure out who did it by sitting her on the porch.

So, after waving goodbye and exchanging a few more pleasantries, I got into my car and headed back on the dirt road. Instead of going left toward my parents' house, though, I turned right toward the outskirts of the city and the Pecan Country Club.

Country Clubs were usually associated with wealth and highfalutin society, but Pecan Country Club was a slapped together, red brick ranch-style building in the center of a few acres of a sad-looking golf course. Complete with cattle fence décor and a pool that was usually crowded with moms and kids, who could pay the one-dollar-a-day fee to escape the summer heat.

While moms gathered at the pool, if Dads weren't on the course, they were usually hanging out by the wooden shed next to the course, aka the booze barn.

So aptly named because it was a large, pier and

beam metal shed that was turned into a bar, complete with whiskey barrel stools, usually occupied by Pecan's finest.

Which meant I had to tread lightly if any of the boys in blue were also hanging around tonight.

Or a certain detective who told me to mind my own beeswax.

But what Mr. Suit didn't know, wouldn't hurt him.

And hopefully not me either.

The wrought iron double doors opened to a small foyer with a linoleum floor in need a of a good scrubbing.

The white textured wall had vinyl letters and an arrow directing you to the left for the bathrooms and the event center and to the right for the bar.

Just about every Pecan dance and wedding took place in the event center, including my own wedding. Even the beautiful view of the golf course and Lake Pecan was overshadowed by Archie spending a little too much time at the open bar and most of the night puking.

Should have been my first clue something was wrong when his Mama took me away from the first dance with my daddy to escort me past rows of our friends to the men's restroom where her son had passed out.

Staring at the metal sign to the left with the word *Cowboy* and a stick figure of a man in a Stetson hat, I swallowed my own thoughts. Trying not to think of the last time I was here.

Now I was on a different mission. One that hopefully didn't end just as badly.

Pivoting in the other direction, I opened the heavy glass door to the bar. The air-conditioning thwapped me in the face, followed by the stench of alcohol and way too much musky cologne.

Nobody had paid any mind to me as I walked in, everyone too busy hanging around the stone bar, their clubs propped up behind them.

I wondered how many of them actually played or were they just camped out on one of the stools, the shiny golf pieces like a hood ornament.

It didn't take long to spot the person I came to see.

Edgar was a man of formidable size, his sides practically flopping off the stool where he perched, laughing, and holding court with the other middle-aged men in sweaty golf polos.

Now that I was actually in the room with the guy, I wished I'd thought of a plan.

If Sophia were here, she would know.

Sophia.

That was the answer.

Before anyone could recognize me, I slipped into a faux leather corner booth, ducking my head down as I pulled my phone out of my purse and brought up Sophia's number.

She might not have been able to come with me, but maybe she'd be able to answer a few SOS texts.

Leslie: Okay, so hypothetically, if I were at the country club bar and a heavily drinking Edgar is here who wanted his deceased brother to sell their land, what would I do?

Sophia: Is this hypothetical or are you actually there and creepy Edgar is asking you to sit on his lap?

Gripping my phone, my chest fell down to my stomach.

Not one of my best ideas, going alone to confront a potential murderer who also was also the creepiest Santa every year at the local VFW Christmas parties.

That place gave me even more of the creeps than this bar.

At least the bar had been built within the last twenty years and someone had kept up the Formica tables. At night, it had a view through the floor-to-ceiling windows looking onto the moon-lit golf club. The VFW was just a squat, metal building a few paces down from Pecan Baptist. No windows. Peeling wood floor. And the scent of cigarette smoke that never left.

Leslie: Yes, okay? I'm here at the golf course. I stopped by Tiffany's and she said something about Edgar and Billy getting into a fight about wanting to sell the ranch land, so I thought I might try and talk to Edgar, but now that I'm actually here...

Sophia: Ugh! I wish I could meet you there but I promised Jake we'd catch up on that new Netflix show when the kids go to bed. And if I don't, he'll watch it without me.

Leslie: So, you're going to ditch me because you're afraid of your husband Netflix-cheating?

Sophia: Hey, you should have asked me to come in the first place.

I sighed, slumping against the bristle padding of the booth.

She was right, of course, but I was so close now.

And someday I had to do things for myself. Guess today was that day.

Aside from needing a few words of encouragement.

Sophia: Okay, so what you need to do is get his attention and have him come to you.

My shoulders straightened as I raised an eyebrow she couldn't see.

Leslie: And how do I do that?

Sophia: Catch his eye and wink.

I shuddered, my skin crawling as if spiders traveled down my arms.

Leslie: You do remember this is Edgar, right?

Sophia: Yes, I know that.

Sophia: And you know that.

Sophia: But he doesn't know that.

Sophia: And if he's drunk, he'll give the information out easy.

Sophia: And think you're bonding and you like him enough that he can trust you.

I groaned, but it did make sense. All of those days of watching crime shows while baking had made Sophia the resident expert. Now if it would actually work in real life and not just on daytime TV…

Leslie: Okay, fine, I'm going to try this, but keeping my keys between my fingers and my thumb on the phone to call. So, don't ignore me if it rings.

Sophia: There's an app you can just use to call 911.

I wasn't going to get the cops involved in this, especially since Detective Adam told me to stay out.

No. This was just going to be me and creepy VFW Santa.

I dragged my phone to my lap as I let out a deep breath.

Okay.

I could do this.

Exactly like Sophia had said.

I hadn't looked at my reflection in the mirror lately and the humidity probably wasn't doing me any favors. My bangs stuck to my forehead and the cold air conditioner ran chills along my scalp where my top knot started.

But this was Edgar in a dark shack of a country club bar. Guess maybe I shouldn't worry as much about my hair. Or what he could see into my tank top and dog-hair-covered-yoga pants.

Sitting up straighter, I trailed my gaze along the bar stools until I landed on Edgar's.

He tipped his head back, gulping the liquid from his stein, magnifying those bloodshot brown eyes.

I wasn't sure he saw me until he plopped the glass on the stone bar top then wiped his mouth with the back of his hand. His gaze never wavering.

Goosebumps prickled the back of my neck as I gulped, forcing a smile. My hand froze in mid-air somewhere between a wave and an air high-five.

Shoot. Shoot. Shoot.

What now? What now?

Edgar nodded to a few of the men with him, mumbling something I couldn't hear from across the bar.

Before I could stealthily grab my keys or put 911 on speed dial, he'd gotten up from his stool and shuffled over.

"Leslie, Leslie, how ya been, honey?" His beefy hand gripped my shoulder, the scent of beer and sweat wafting off of him.

I tried not to wince or pull away from his grip, forcing a smile at the way he said 'honey' just a little too leery for my liking.

I should have maybe put on something other

than a tank top and my cut off yoga pants, but it was still in the high nineties past sundown, and I couldn't bear to think about putting on anything else.

But now that his blood shot eyes raked over my small expanse of a chest and down my legs, I was starting to regret this decision even more.

Swallowing hard, I straightened my shoulders, trying to appear tough, yet relaxed.

"I think I'm the one who should be asking you that."

Without permission, he leaned in closer before plopping down next to me in the booth, the leather material releasing a loud gust of air beneath his weight.

"Thank you for saying that yanno, it's been rough with Billy's funeral coming up, but a man just isn't supposed to mourn over his brother."

Now came the water works, little droplets dribbling down his face that he wiped with the back of his hand.

Dang it, I needed to get better at this emotional stuff.

Maybe I should have patted him on the back or used some encouraging words.

But all I could do was sit there straight as a

board, opening and closing my mouth as I tried to think of the right thing to say.

"Billy and I had our differences, but he was still my big brother."

Large snot bubbles hiccupped out of his nose, and like everything else that came out of his nose and mouth, he wiped with them the back of his hand.

"It's not your fault, Edgar," I said gently, reaching to put my hand on his then remembered the dried snot and quickly pulled back.

He sniffled before clearing his throat. "Yeah, that's what Susan keeps saying, too, but she wasn't the one who fought with him and now my brother's dead. Oh god, my brother's dead."

He covered his wails with his hands, garnering a few stares from nearby patrons at the bar side-eyeing us hard.

Okay, not the reaction I was expecting.

"We all fight with our siblings," I said in an attempt to commiserate. "I remember fighting with my brother all the time about stupid things when we were younger."

My brother, Cash, who barely even called me anymore, too busy with his family somewhere in the

Midwest to ever visit, no matter how much Ma prodded.

But if Cash showed up dead in a hot tub after one of our arguments about spending Christmas in Pecan…I don't know what my reaction would be.

I wished Sophia were with me, she'd know what to say to prod Edgar in this situation and not have guilt riddling her stomach.

Was Edgar faking his grief? How would I even challenge that.

I was the worst person to talk to about family issues.

Edgar sniffled, wiping another long line of snot along the hairs on his arm. I had to look down at the tabletop.

"Look, Billy and I had our arguments, especially recently that all them developers were wanting the land. But I wouldn't kill my brother for it. You believe me, right?"

He paused, the sound of his sniffles ringing in my ears.

I looked up to meet those blood shot eyes, trying to figure out if he really was telling me the truth. "No one is saying you killed him, Edgar."

He frowned. "Tell that to my sister-in-law. She thinks just because we fought over some land that those developers wanted that I'd go off on him. Pft. That woman didn't know the half of our situation."

I sat a little straighter, my ears perking.

"Yeah?"

He nodded, thumping his fingers on the table. "This stays between you and me?"

I swallowed hard. "Yeah. Sure."

He sucked in a breath then let it out slowly. "Billy and I made arrangements that he was going to buy the rest of the land from me. Not to sell, but because I'd gotten in a bit of trouble with the old card games up in Durant and needed the money fast, before Susan found out. We were going to head to the lawyer's office this weekend and now…"

Tears welled up in his eyes. "And now instead we'll be going to my brother's funeral."

Bingo.

The tips of my ears burned as I tried not to smile.

Okay, so this was a little bit more of a hint.

Who would want to stop them?

My mind raced for answers as I let him quietly sob into his drink for a while, exchanging a few niceties before I was able to excuse myself and he was called back to his buddies.

As soon as I was out of the bar, I pulled up

Sophia's name on my phone. My heart was thumping so loudly in my chest, I swore it vibrated through my whole body and onto the gravel.

She probably wouldn't answer, but I thought a text would work.

But what would I say without being suspicious?

A glaring light caught my phone, and I tried to shield it with my hand as I stepped forward.

Tires squealed against gravel as I looked up just in time to barely miss the front end of a golf cart.

Though my head and the gravel below didn't fare so well.

10

I told Edgar and the rest of the patrons not to call an ambulance.

Multiple times, even if my words were a bit slurred, and I couldn't sit up from my face down position in the gravel path.

But of course, no one listened to me, especially since the world was spinning around me, and I wasn't exactly sure which way was up when the patrons at the bar all came barreling out, screaming my name.

Sitting in the back of the ambulance while the EMTs, all whom I'm fairly sure I babysat in high school, checked out the back of my head, I wondered how the heck I even got here.

And who would try to run me over.

No one came forward saying it was an accident and they didn't see me.

The world went dark as soon as the front end of the golf cart came crashing toward me.

No plates or markings I could recognize.

None I would have even looked for.

Glancing at Edgar out of the corner of my eye, the man was still sobbing as he talked to one of the local police officers.

Had he been crying since I left?

Or was that just a front?

I sucked in a breath, my heart beating in my ears either from a concussion or the questioning in my brain.

How long was I outside?

How long would it take Edgar to leave the booth and come around to the side, getting his golf cart to knock me off course and not rouse suspicion.

Someone who knew exactly where I would be and when.

I glanced at the bar patrons who had gathered outside only for a few minutes then went back to their stools. But I did notice the blinds still open, many of them peeking out to make sure they didn't miss a thing.

Sometimes the men were bigger gossips than the women.

But with my pounding headache and scratched up arms, I didn't care about the gossip.

Right now, I just wanted the pain to go away and to know who the heck was doing this.

The cold chill returned to prickle the back of my neck.

If it wasn't Edgar, who else knew I'd be here at the golf course?

Who wouldn't want me to find out about the land and the family arguments?

"Oh, honey, there you are," Ma's voice cooed over the EMT's before her hands started flapping like a chicken without her eggs.

"Ma, I told you, I'm fine. Just a little bit bruised up."

Though that was partially the truth.

My mind was going a mile a minute.

Who had access to the golf carts?

Who would want to run me over or scare me?

The same person who killed Billy?

"She's right, a few bruises, but a possible concussion, so you'll want to keep an eye on that," one of the baby-faced EMTs said.

Ma pulled out her phone, tapping at the keys

with manicured fingers. "How do you spell concussion?"

"Ma'am, you don't need to Google it, actually we'd prefer if you didn't," Another EMT replied.

Ma huffed, putting her hands on her hips as she narrowed her eyes at the man, if you could even call him that. "Johnny Gonzalez, I changed your diapers in the church nursery. Don't you try and sass me." His slicked back, dark hair and horn-rimmed glasses hadn't saved him from Mom's scalding lecture.

The lights may have been dim, but I swore Johnny's cheeks blushed bright red as the other EMT snickered.

"Sorry to interrupt this cheerful reunion."

I froze as a familiar deep voice perked my ears.

Even scarier than the thought of someone following me out of the bar was that of a certain man who told me to stay away from it all.

The neon lights of the bar illuminated half of the detective's face. The five o'clock shadow and bleary eyes that said he'd either just woken up or spent way too many late nights at the office.

His cold stare was aimed right in my direction. "But I have a few questions for Miss Winters."

Ma's hand fluttered to her chest as her eyes

roamed over the detective from his shiny dress shoes to his dark blue suit, pressing over broad shoulders.

I may have had a possible concussion, but I wasn't blind to a good-looking man. A good-looking man staring daggers in my direction.

And apparently neither was my ma.

"My, I believe we haven't met, sir. I'm Miss Winters' mother, Ann Marie Winters, and you are?" She batted her eyelashes and it took everything I had not to roll my eyes, but that probably would have made the dull ache in the back of my head worse.

He cleared his throat. "Detective Adam Waltz, Dallas PD."

Ma blinked hard, her voice raising with each word. "Oh, my, a detective? What questions do you have for my daughter? Do you think someone was out to hurt her? The same person who shot Mr. Williams?"

He frowned. "Ma'am, that's part of an ongoing investigation, and if you and the EMTs wouldn't mind, I'd like to have a few words with Miss Winters. Privately."

"Don't need to tell us twice," Johnny muttered, grabbing his gear as the other guy followed suit. They headed to one of the Pecan trees where they each pulled out a pack of Marlboros from their pockets.

Should EMTs have been smoking?

I guess after dealing with my mama, I'd want a smoke, too.

"Mrs. Winters, I'm gonna have to ask you to give us a little privacy as well." The detective eyed Ma and if he thought that was going to work, well, it was obvious he'd never been a teenage girl with a mama who didn't know the word privacy.

"Oh, well, Leslie, I'll be right over here if you need me." Ma nodded, looking from the detective and back to me before shooting me a wink.

Oh Geez, as if my night couldn't get any worse.

Since when did she start listening to people about minding her own business?

Ma strode off toward a group of workers who had gathered to watch the commotion, keeping one eye on us. I mentally prepared myself for the barrage of questions later about the detective.

But first, I had to deal with the man himself, staring me down with that perpetual frown. "I feel like we just had a conversation about you staying out of this investigation, Miss Winters."

"Can't a girl just have a drink at the local country club without getting run over?" I folded my arms across my chest, trying to widen my eyes and project some extra innocence.

But my efforts didn't not even garner a smile from the detective. "And that drink included you having a conversation with the brother of a crime victim?"

I narrowed my eyes. How fast did news travel around here?

"We've already talked to Mr. Williams. He said he saw you at a corner booth and you two just talked about his brother. But my question is, why would you show up on the local men's golf league night without a set of clubs and after dark?"

I threw my hands in the air in a huff. "What do you want me to say, Detective? That I came here hoping for some answers? Well, I did. And now I'm even more confused than I was when I got here, and I have a headache to boot. Happy now?"

He sighed, taking a step forward. A wave of a woodsy cologne rolled off of him, surrounding my senses like a warm blanket that I could just breathe in.

"Miss Winters…"

"Leslie. I've told you to call me Leslie."

"Leslie." He took another step closer until we

were toe-to-toe then slowly he slid down to take a seat at the back of the ambulance next to me.

His elbow rubbed against mine, by accident? On purpose? Whatever it was, I tried to ignore the goose bumps that prickled across my skin.

"Did anyone know you were coming here tonight?" He pulled a small notebook out of his pocket, flipping it open and then procured a pen from that same pocket.

Did people still carry those? I thought those were reserved for old spy movies.

I swallowed hard, shaking my head. "No, I just left Tiffany Williams' place after dropping off a covered dish and thought I'd stop by for a drink before picking up some stuff at the Dollar General."

Not a complete lie, yet by the detective's smirk, I had a feeling he was starting to catch on to me.

"Tiffany Williams? You go and see her a lot?"

I huffed, my head now pounding. "Am I a suspect now, detective?"

The smirk disappeared from his face as he raised his eyebrows, looking up from the notepad.

"There is someone else out there that doesn't want you getting involved in this. Someone that could be extremely dangerous to your well-being if tonight is any indication. I'm going to have a local officer post up at your house for a few days. Just to make sure nothing else happens."

I shook my head. "You don't need to do that. The town is strapped enough with a small force."

His hand went to mine, the warmth knocking the next words right out of me. "Leslie, I want to make sure you're safe, okay. Can you just try to lay low for a while? Stop this sleuthing and let me and my team handle this?"

My tongue twisted as I searched for the right words.

"Promise?" He squeezed my hand, which did nothing to calm my nerves.

All I could do was nod in response, though, I did have my legs crossed, so that didn't count as a promise, right?

11

A possible concussion means you're supposed to stay awake. Like all the time.

And when your parents volunteer to stay up with you to make sure you don't fall and drift into a coma, they both promptly pass out on their respective recliners within the first hour of your re-run binge.

So, while they were snoring away, I pried my eyes open with toothpicks and pulled out my phone, prepared for a mindless scroll of social media.

But then a text popped up from the last person I wanted to talk to.

Archie: Are you okay? Mom said you were in some sort of accident.

My temples throbbed, and I wasn't sure if it was

from the concussion or just hearing that my ex-mother-in-law had already gotten the news from the gossip mill and told her darling son.

The question was…did he really care? What did my ex-husband really want?

He wasn't like the detective. He didn't sit there and tell me he was looking out for me. Heck, Archie didn't do that for anyone, not even Bandit.

I should have ignored him like I had every other call trying to pry some insider information from me, but with nothing on TV but old reruns of History Channel shows, I figured an argument with my ex would at least keep me up for a while.

Leslie: I'm fine. Not that it's any of your business.

Archie: Of course, it's my business. You've been ignoring my calls and texts for days. Is something going on I should know about? Is Bandit okay?

Glancing down at my lap, my little Dashie had found a way to curl his furry body between the arm of the couch and my elbow. Not the most comfortable position for me, but I wasn't going to move the snoring pup.

And instead of answering my ex's stupid question, I just sent a picture of Bandit.

Archie: Man, I can't wait to see him again.

Leslie: Uh, who says you're going to see him again?

Archie: Well, if you'd answer my phone calls, you'd know that Stephie and I are moving to Pecan to be closer to my parents and hers who live in Dallas.

I opened and closed my mouth, turning away from the screen then looking again.

Surely, I wasn't reading that right.

And what kind of grown woman goes by the name 'Stephie'? Especially the grown woman who was going to have my ex's baby?

Archie: Take it you're shocked and not going to answer. Well, you should have answered my phone calls when I tried to tell you.

Archie: Already put in for a transfer to the real estate office in Rockwall and made a deposit on a new build in Caddo. We'll be in next week before the wedding, which I'm sure Mom's already told you about, if not Sophia, who I'm sure Mom already contacted about making the cake.

As if things couldn't get any worse, tears pricked my eyes.

My ex had moved on with his new life. And that new life was now going to be right here in Pecan.

I needed a drink. Or maybe a pint of Bluebell I was sure Dad had hidden in the back of the fridge.

But I got the second-best thing with a group text initiated by Piper.

Probably the gossip mill had hit her quick and she wanted details.

Well, I guess it was better than talking to Archie.

I sucked in a breath and let it out slowly.

Well, I guess I had nothing better to do.

Piper: Hey y'all. It was good to see y'all at Awanas the other night but didn't have much time to chat. Tad is working late tomorrow so thought maybe y'all wanted to come over for happy hour. You can bring the kids, Sophia, mine will be running around.

I blinked, reading the words over once then twice, making sure my mind wasn't playing tricks on me.

Happy Hour?

Did Baptists even do that?

Heck, I could definitely use it though. Especially after this conversation with Archie

Sophia: Hey, I could always use a break and happy hour sounds good to me. Should I make a double batch of mini lemon tarts?

Piper: Um, yeah! Sounds amazing. Are you in, Leslie?

Immediately my phone buzzed with a text from Sophia.

Sophia: Hey, Jake just fell asleep in the middle of our show #typical. But did you see Piper's message? Do you think she just wants the gossip about what happened tonight? Because, you know I do.

I sighed, hovering my fingers over the buttons.

I had a million things to say to my best friend and none I wanted to do while I still had this massive headache.

Leslie: Like how I just got a text from Archie asking if his mama talked to you about making the cake for him and Stephie's wedding?

Sophia: WHAT? No, she didn't contact me. That dragon lady, I bet she's using the new baker in Caddo. Not that I'd do it for her anyway, but grrrr. Okay, now we definitely need to meet up because this. Well, this is a heckuva lot.

Bandit nudged my arm with his paw, then with his nose, the universal symbol for 'pay attention to me, human'. He rolled onto his back, placing his paws in the air, and looked at me with those beady little eyes, demanding me to rub his belly.

Setting my phone down on the arm rest, I reached down and gave him a good scratch on his puffed chest, his eyes going to half-mast as he gave a satisfied snort.

"Maybe I should just take you with me to all my investigating, huh? You wouldn't let anything happen to your human, would you? And probably better company if Archie happens to come around."

He gave me another snort in response.

Before I could stop myself, I figured I'd blame it on the possible concussion and conversation with Archie later, I sent my reply to the ladies.

Leslie: I'm in, but can I bring Bandit?

———

The next evening, Bandit lolled his head out the passenger window while I sipped on an extreme cappuccino I bought at the gas station where I filled up. Together, we bounded down the gravel road toward the Drake compound hoping for a break. In the case. In my life. In our luck. I'd take whatever I could get.

Piper, her mom, sister, and uncles, all lived on the same crepe myrtle-lined street. Her uncle built the property for his church back in the 1960s, but after the church moved to their bigger location in town, the Drake's remained on the property. Rumor had it the church was haunted by the ghost of the former Auntie Dixie Drake. She had a thing for twisting kid's pinkies when they didn't pay attention in Sunday school.

Not that I believed in ghosts, but I did say a small prayer when I passed the old church and pulled into the driveway of Piper's Mediterranean style home, a stark contrast to the Texas ranch style homes before it.

Rumor had it that Piper's husband, Tad, didn't want to build on her family's property, but Piper's dad made him an offer he couldn't refuse.

They settled on making their house unique by adding in a large inground pool surrounded by a privacy fence so Tad didn't have to look at his mother-in-law's evil glare when he went for a swim.

Or enjoy a happy hour, which, from the twang of country music blaring over the fence and the light of the tiki torches, might already be in full swing.

Briefly, my mind flitted to my conversation with Archie. I wondered if his mama would demand they build on their property like she wanted us to do after we got married. Archie defied her by moving to Houston.

The party sounds drew me closer. I really needed this happy hour now that my ex was coming back and a murderer in town might also have me in his sights. Or hers.

Bandit and I rounded the back of the house, and my spirits lifted when I spotted the top of Sophia's blonde bun over the top of the fence. I unlocked the gate with one hand and juggled my store bought fruit tray with the other.

Inside the patio, Sophia's kids mingled with Piper's two little girls. The sun-kissed cuties laughed and splashed in the kidney-shaped pool while Sophia perched at a bamboo bar waiting for Piper to finish mixing some concoction in a blender.

"Hey, you made it!" Piper called to me before the whirl of the blender started up.

"Wow, this is some set up," I said, air-kissing Sophia as I placed the fruit tray on the bar.

I'd always imagined having a resort-type back-yard like this with a pool, waterfall, and full wet bar.

Archie showed me homes like this listed in Houston. After his "next big commission" we'd get one, he'd always say.

Too bad that the "we" turned out to be Archie and Stephie. And his promised big commission scored their soon to be house in Caddo.

"Oh, honey, you look like you could use a drink."

I blinked into reality when Piper, showing off her cheerleader form in a revealing one-piece bathing suit, thrust a plastic cup full of some kind of yellow and red slush.

Bandit balanced on his back paws, his nose high in the air as he took in the scent of coconut and strawberries wafting through the blender.

"Sorry, pup, I don't think this is doggie food." I scratched his ears before taking a seat at one of the wrought iron stools.

He reluctantly plopped down on the cement, still looking up at me with those beady black eyes like maybe, just maybe I'd feel bad enough to give him a taste.

"What is this?" I asked, turning back toward the

ladies. I sniffed the rim, not getting any hint of alcohol in the pink and yellow swirly concoction.

"Miami Vices. Tad and I had them on our cruise last year, and I've been thinking about them for days. I picked up some stuff last night and thought what better than a happy hour to try out the recipe?"

Sophia already had gulped half of hers before I could even take the first sip, the sugary liquid hitting my tastebuds without the usual burn of alcohol.

"Wow, these are good. Compliments to the chef."

I raised my glass and Piper raised hers, along with Sophia, and like the Three Musketeers, we clinked the plastic cups together.

Sophia gave me a look, raising an eyebrow as I took another tiny sip of my drink.

Probably still not the best idea to drink too many of anything with a recent head injury, but they were too delicious to resist. Like the slushies we got at Sonic. Couldn't even taste any alcohol. Which I would have questioned if I didn't see the half-empty handle of rum on the counter near the blender.

"So, what have y'all been up to?" Piper asked,

plopping down on the bar stool between me and Sophia.

I glanced at Bandit, happily at my feet, a safe distance from the kids he studied squirting each other with water guns. "Oh, you know, work and all that."

The usual Worried about an ex moving back and a killer after me..

Sophia and Piper talked about their kids' activities, and I chimed in when I could, continuing to sip on my drink until the fuzzy effects of the alcohol seeped in and I finally relaxed against the leather back of my seat.

Piper jumped up, shaking her empty cup. "Y'all ready for a refill?"

"Sure," Sophia said, smacking her lips together way too enthusiastically. She glanced at me out of the corner of her eye with raised eyebrows. We both knew there was a conversation we needed to have, but now wasn't the time.

Piper blended up another batch of her concoction filling our cups to the rim.

She waited until we took our first gulps and sat back down before she spoke again.

"Now that you're a bit more relaxed, it's time for me to tell you why I asked y'all here."

My shoulders tensed as I tried to somehow sober myself up, readying myself for the conversation.

Should have known this was coming.

Sophia batted her eyelashes. "You didn't just want our fabulous company?"

Piper rolled her eyes. "Not that this isn't nice, but I know what y'all are doing with the Williams investigation, and I want in."

I took a large gulp of my drink, trying to come up with the words that were stuck in my throat.

"What...what are you talking about? Investigation? We aren't detectives or anything," Sophia flustered through her words.

"Oh, please. I know y'all aren't cops. But I know you're doing some sleuthing, asking questions around Awana's and after what Tad said happened last night on the golf course to you, Leslie, y'all are in over your heads and could use the help of the town gossip."

"Well...I wasn't going to call you that..." I muttered.

She put one hand on her hip, straightening her posture as she adjusted the straps of her tie-dye swim suit cover-up. "Look, we can just sit here and talk about the weather and high school football and pretend this never happened, or I can tell you what I know about Miss Haley Williams and you can tell me what you talked to Edgar about at the country club."

My ears burned as my mind battled with itself.

Detective Adam had said to stop sleuthing.

But was it sleuthing if I was just having a neighborly conversation with two friends by the pool and not thinking about my ex?

Even if said two friends may have been talking about people related to a murder?

"You go first," Sophia blurted.

Piper poked her straw at her drink, taking a big slurp before she gave us an innocent gaze like she hadn't engineered this whole get together for this very moment. "Okay. Fine."

She folded her hands together on her lap, smacking her lips together. "Word got around that Miss Haley wasn't staying at Tiffany's. Because she's staying at her girlfriend's house in Dallas."

Tell me something I don't already know, Piper I said to myself. Tiffany had told me Haley stayed at a friend's house the night of the murder.

"Her girlfriend, *girl*friend," Piper added, raising her eyebrows high on her head.

"You mean Haley…?" Sophia asked slowly.

Piper nodded. "Guess she was her college room-mate. Haley finally told her daddy right before he passed that she wanted to move in with the girl, and her daddy was none too happy."

I blinked hard, trying to process the words in my fuzzy brain. "How did you even hear about this?" I asked, willing the effects of Piper's drink to bypass my processing faculties.

She smirked. "Well, aside from the local gossip train, all you have to do is pull up Haley's name on any social media site. Those pictures of her and her," Piper paused to air quote friend as though Sophia and I were too thick to get her meaning, "*friend* don't exactly look like anything I would take with someone I was just shooting the breeze with at happy hour, if you know what I mean."

Sophia and I both grabbed our phones, each pulling up a different app and searching Haley's name.

The hair on the back of my neck stood on end as I scrolled through Haley's photos. I couldn't miss the curvy blonde in the forefront of each image. Some snapshots were just close ups with Haley and her unnamed friend smiling along the streets of Dallas. Others showed a bit more intimate relationship, from hand holding to a kiss that should have come with a warning label for heat.

Quickly, I slid my phone back down on the bar, but Sophia scrolled through a few more items before she did the same.

"Okay, so Haley is a lesbian. It's a modern time, right?" Sophia said, her words a bit slurred.

Piper tilted her chin forward. "Yeah, but you know Billy. Do you really think he'd be okay with his daughter being with another woman?"

I shook my head, wondering how far Billy's eyes had bugged out of his head when he heard the news and how many curse words flew around. Between Haley and her dad when she came out of the closet.

"But would she kill him because of it…?" I said, asking the question we were all thinking.

"The only way to know is to ask," Piper replied.

"And how in the heck are we supposed to do that? Show up to one of the bars uptown? Jake will kill me if I'm out past the kids' bedtimes," Sophia added, slurping up the last frothy drops of her drink.

"The funeral and luncheon are this weekend. No way Haley won't be there, and if the girlfriend is in tow, there will be a lot of questions. And maybe, just maybe they'll both need an escape for their own happy hour." Piper held up her glass, sloshing the slush around.

"You can be pretty persuasive with a bit of liquor." Sophia nodded.

"Happy hour by my pool, some of Sophia's famous chocolate chip cookies, and the sympathetic ear of a friend who went through a similar experience should do the trick." Piper batted her eye lashes at me.

This was my cue to back away now. Make up some lie about needing to be home so I wouldn't worry my parents.

But instead, I opened my mouth and poured out everything about the night with Edgar as we plotted our new plan to figure out who was behind the death of Billy Williams.

12

I said an extra silent prayer on the way to the funeral home in town.

Surely, I'd be forgiven for questioning a dead man's daughter at his burial if it were for the greater good of finding his killer.

Wallace Funeral Home was right off the Pecan town square, across from the post office. In part because it was the only funeral home within a twenty-mile radius, it had a better-kept parking lot and brick facade than most of the other buildings in the square, but also thanks to the older population, who kept it frequently booked.

That and some of the younger population who thought it would be a great trip thirty minutes north to the canyon and dare their friends to jump into the river below.

Rest in peace to so many of the class of 1993.

After squeezing my SUV next to a minivan in the last available spot at the funeral home, I took one last look in my passenger seat covered in dog fur.

Maybe I should have brought Bandit, even if he just sat in the passenger seat with the AC on and bird sounds playing from my phone into the speakers.

He may have been small, but the dog could hear or smell something coming from at least a mile away and warn me.

But surely no one would try to run me over at a funeral?

Didn't think anyone would run me over ever… but…here we are.

A knock at my window almost knocked the bun out of my hair.

Sophia stood by the door, in her signature black maxi dress she wore for Christmas Eve church service and funerals. The same thing she'd worn since we were in high school. Same mud stains on the hem and all.

And that's why we were best friends, because

she was one of the few people in Pecan who wouldn't whisper about my own black dress, borrowed from Ma's closet and possibly not worn since the eighties judging by the balloon sleeves and lingering smell of aerosol hairspray.

"You okay? You look like you've seen a ghost," Sophia said, looking over her shoulder. "Can you see those now? Is that a thing? Do you have psychic abilities?"

I sighed, opening the door, and slid out of the car. "Unless the ghost of Prom Nights Past is somehow attached to this dress, then no."

We walked in step through the gravel parking lot lost in thought until she said, "I like the look. Vintage is coming back, isn't it? And, hey, it'll be a good talking point."

I raised an eyebrow. "Talking point? This is a funeral, not a presidential debate."

She leaned in close, lowering her voice. Her flip flops thwapping against the cobblestone path leading up to the cement stairs of the funeral home.

"When else would we talk to Haley? And what about bother than your dress and if she whacked her dad because of her lesbian lover."

"You watched another one of those old medical shows again last night, didn't you? Coroners with flip phones or the girl who has the dreams?"

She blew a raspberry. "Both. Had a hard time sleeping."

"They give you any other advice on how NOT to talk to people?"

She shrugged before adjusting her hair, undoing, and redoing the big blonde bun. "No, but there was an interesting plot point involving a sister, who framed the lesbian lover. Does Haley have a sister?"

I shook my head. "Not unless you count the dogs."

"Well, there goes that theory," she muttered.

As soon as we opened the double doors to the funeral home, we were hit with the heavy scent of formaldehyde and floral perfume.

The monotony of black dresses and suits in the dark-paneled lobby was broken up by Piper as she pushed through the crowd. She ran toward us like a mad gym teacher in her bright orange shorts and white CrossFit shirt, clashing with the green carpet and smattering of floral settees that had been there since the place opened up in the 1950's.

"There you two are," Piper hissed as a few onlookers whispered before pretending to be engrossed in one of the oil paintings on the wall.

"Did we miss a CrossFit game in the parking lot?" Sophia asked, looking over each shoulder.

Piper rolled her eyes. "I came right after my workout because I thought y'all would be here early, too. I've already gone through the visitation line and had time to pick my Fantasy Football players this week. Where have y'all been?"

"Hey, I was here almost on time...only about ten minutes late, pretty good for me," Sophia said, sitting primly with her hands on her hips.

"Sorry..." It was all I could think of to say.

The last funeral I went to was my Great Mee-Maw's when I was four. I didn't remember much but a lot of crying and a fire and brimstone preacher from south Texas who spoke in tongues.

I barely knew Great Mee-Maw or what was going on. Ma wouldn't let me near the casket, afraid seeing her dead would give me nightmares.

Well, I'd already seen Mr. Williams after he met his maker in nothing but a small bathing suit and his hat, and I wasn't too keen on remembering that.

"There are still seats in the back. Come on." Piper hitched her thumb over her shoulder then whirled back to the oak doors leading inside the funeral home.

Collages and photos of Mr. Williams with his

friends and family lined easels as on-lookers shared stories or paid their respect by laying flowers under the photos.

Those who weren't in the overflowing rows of gray chairs facing the white casket at least, framed in floral bouquets and the pink-curtained walls that really needed to be dusted.

Mr. Williams' Stetson stallion hat peered over the open casket, along with a Texas flag and University of Texas Longhorns banner, placed strategically in his folded hands.

"That is the most Texas thing I've ever seen," Sophia muttered as we took our seats in the last row.

"You should have seen my Paw Paw's funeral. Full longhorn skull in each flower arrangement," Piper added with a nod as if it were the most normal thing in the world.

Note to self: make sure my will states no longhorn skulls or corpse holding flags at my funeral.

"You should hear what they're planning for the graveside service," the young woman in front of us whispered over her shoulder.

"Really?" Sophia leaned forward, her nose almost colliding with the woman's large blonde curls, almost as big as her face.

While most of the people sitting around us wore slacks or old sundresses, this girl was done up with her Texas curls, a black skirt suit, and those fancy heels with the red backs that cost people a fortune.

Nothing about her screamed Pecan local, especially her lack of any frown lines, her baby face, bright blue eyes, and false black lashes said her demographic was definitely of not from around these parts.

"Yeah, Hales said her crazy stepmom hired the church's men's choir to perform 'Deep in the Heart of Texas' while they lower his casket".

The young woman turned her way too cute, upturned nose toward us. "Y'all aren't some of Tiffany's friends, are you?"

I shook my head. "Well, not exactly. More friends of the family. I'm Leslie, the local dog groomer."

The woman put her manicured hand to her chest. "Oh, you poor thing, Hales told me about the last time she saw you. If I weren't worried about causing a scene, I'd get up and hug you right now."

"Why would you cause a scene?" Piper asked, way too eager.

If she were one of my clients, I would have given her a few squirts of the hose to calm down.

The blonde looked over each shoulder before letting out a small breath through her nose. "Miss Tiffany isn't too happy I'm here anyway, but the only way Hales said she'd come was if I did, and god forbid Miss Tiffany look worse than she already does to everyone in Pecan."

"Guess Miss Tiffany isn't fond of Hales' friends?" Piper asked, but before the words escaped her lips, a warning bell had already gone off in my head.

There was something familiar about this blonde, and I couldn't quite put my finger on it.

Did I groom her dogs?

No…

Dallas.

Blonde.

Professional Looking.

Oh no…

The blonde smiled. "Something like that."

Then she turned back to face the front as the preacher started talking to Haley and Tiffany who stood beside the casket.

Sophia raised an eyebrow.

I opened my mouth to speak then thought better of it, pulling out my phone and adding both women on a group text.

.   .   .

Leslie: I think that might be Haley's infamous girlfriend.

Piper: What? No. She doesn't look like she's a...um...

Sophia: Lesbian. Likes girls. Lady lover?

Piper: You knew what I meant! How do we know that's her?

Leslie: It makes sense. She said Tiffany didn't want her here and Haley's high school friends are a few rows ahead. Even her old chess team isn't sitting near this girl. So why wouldn't Haley's friends sit with her either?

Sophia: Why don't you ask her?

Leslie: I can't just ask while a preacher is about to talk.

Sophia: Maybe we'll get a hint at the cemetery.

Piper: If we can survive the men's choir's off-key rendition of Deep in the Heart of Texas.

———

Pecan Cemetery was not even two miles from the funeral home, butting right up against the country club and golf course.

Which, of course, had me glancing over my shoulder for any rogue carts as we parked along the gravel path.

Pecan Cemetery was considered a historical landmark with graves dating back to the civil war. In the distance, on a clear dear, you could even spot Crab Apple Canyon as the sun hit the very tops of the rolling hills.

But on this cloudy day, all you could see was Texas pride with the red, white, and blue flags waving all over the tent where Mr. Williams' bright white casket set against a landscape of green grass and yellow tulips.

"There's Haley and Tiffany," Piper whispered as we made our way to the tent with the other patrons.

I did not intend to actually go to the graveside service. I was just paying my respects at the funeral home, but my friends were right. There was something off about the blonde girl's presence and maybe here we'd find out why.

"Leslie, should have expected to see you here," a deep drawl purred.

One that had me wincing like a kid caught cheating on a math test. Which I had; too bad Sophia was just as bad as me in all of our math classes during school.

Sophia and Piper whipped their heads around, but I moved a bit slower. I sucked in a breath, trying to let it out slowly as I finally faced the detective Clad in a dark black suit, nicer than anything any of the other men were wearing, the man gave a whole new meaning to the term tall, dark and handsome.

And the suit fit better in the shoulders and down his tapered waist than most of theirs did too.

Not that I was noticing.

"Paying my respects like everyone else," I said with the biggest smile I could muster under the circumstances.

"Not trying anymore of that amateur detective work, are you?"

I balked at his words, putting my hand to my heavy beating heart as if I were offended. "How dare you say that at a funeral of a respected man in Pecan,"

The well-dressed detective rolled his mesmerizing eyes. "You and I both know of the bad blood going on in this town, and you're probably going to tell me you've already talked to Miss Rangor up there all about where she was the day of Mr. Williams death."

"Miss who now?"

He blinked hard, taking a step back.

Good, he was taken off guard and his face definitely clued that in.

He cleared his throat, looking at the crowd.

I followed his gaze to the petite blonde from the church.

And I mean really petite.

Sitting down, she looked tiny, but now, even in heels, she was almost a head shorter than everyone else.

"Oh, Haley's girlfriend. So that's her name."

He blinked again slowly. If this man had a tell, this was it.

Bingo.

"Yeah, she had some interesting things to say about Haley's stepmother."

Before he could respond, the men's choir gathered in front of the casket.

Men ranging from about mid-sixties to close to one hundred. All in their best black suits and Stetson hats.

One man, crouched over a knobbed wooden

cane pulled a harmonica from his pocket, playing a few chords before the men started in an off-key rendition of "Deep in the Heart of Texas".

"Okay, Leslie, you win," the detective grumbled.

I almost couldn't hear him over several attempted high notes, but knew as soon as I glanced at his frown, my heart rate sped up, knowing that something big was going to happen.

"What? I win? You want to join the men's choir?"

He sighed, pressing the bridge of his nose before leaning closer to me.

His eyes darted around before he finally spoke. "You give me what you talked about with Miss Rangor, and I might dangle a little carrot in your own gossip mill."

I scoffed, but my ears had perked up. "There's no gossip mill."

A laugh caught in his chest, shaking his shoulders as they vibrated against my dress. He was so close I could smell his manly cologne and feel the heat radiating off his body. And, heck, it was hot enough already with the humidity.

"Which is why you, the cookie lady, and the cheer coach are all here together, asking a lot of questions."

"I would never. You told me to stay out of this," I said innocently, trying to ignore my heart now beating in my ears.

"So I take it you wouldn't want to know about the questions I asked Miss Rangor this morning about her whereabouts the other day."

I froze, my heart thudding hard in my chest as my brain racked with what he was saying.

Did I give into the bait?

Sophia and Piper glanced over their shoulder, their eyebrows raised.

On one hand, the detective could be setting a trap for me.

On the other...

"Okay, you go first," I said.

He did the silent laugh again.

"Nice try."

I blew a raspberry, weighing my options and, well, I didn't have any.

"Miss Rangor, as you called her, doesn't get along with Tiffany. Who didn't want her here."

"Interesting."

I scowled, glancing at him over my shoulder after making sure no one else was keen on our conversation? "What? Expecting me to say she confessed to a murder in the ball room with a knife?"

"No, just that when I spoke to her this morning, she said she had no quarrel with Mrs. Williams."

I snorted, covering my mouth so no one turned around, thinking I was disrespecting the men's choir.

"Quarrel? Were those her words? Bless her heart."

"Maybe not those exact words, but you get the picture," he grumbled, keeping his focus on the men's choir who now had half the men blubbering as they just kept on singing.

"Yeah, I get that you meet the girlfriend of a small-town girl from Texas and expect no one will have a problem when the closet flies wide open for everyone and their mamas to see at a funeral."

He nodded. "You're right. And Miss Rangor is a Dallas professional with a lot of social and some questionable ties."

"What are you saying?" If I had Spidey senses, they'd be tingling.

"Just be careful, okay?"

I fully turned to face him, not caring that the men's choir was still going on or that my manners would be questioned later.

"You think she's after me? She didn't even know who I was before today, and I doubt she would be able to get into a golf cart, let alone reach the pedals."

His dark eyes bore into me as he leaned forward, his voice low as the spicy scent of his cologne and the leather of his jacket filled my senses.

"Like I said, she has some questionable ties and powerful friends. Not to mention a grandpa who is a former police chief who would have carried a similar gun to the one found at the Williams ranch."

I swallowed hard, quickly flitting my gaze to the grass as I turned back around.

Why would Haley's girlfriend do this?

Did she really not know who I was or was she just playing innocent?

As the men's choir finished singing, everyone rose for the preacher.

Looking through the crowd, I found a small opening where Haley sat next to Tiffany.

Her hand behind her back and clasping onto a perfectly manicured one.

Her girlfriend's.

Between her sniffles, Tiffany's eyes would

narrow, glaring at Haley before she finally leaned in and whispered to her step-daughter.

Haley didn't say a word, just let go of her girl-friend's hand before crossing her arms over her lap.

Miss Rangor stared for a long time at the back of Tiffany's Texas curls before leaning back in her seat.

Could this girl really be part of some evil master plan?

There was only one way to find out, and there was no way I was going to let Detective Adam Waltz know.

But just in case he was right about her being dangerous, I figured I needed back up.

And not just the gossip mill kind.

This was a job for whiskey.

13

As the funeral ended, people huddled around the cemetery, hugging Tiffany, or standing near the casket, whispering their silent prayers, some all-out bawling. Yes, Edgar was all out bawling and had to be pulled off by a huffing Susan.

But one person hadn't moved a muscle. And I made a beeline for that person.

"Hey, Miss Rangor, is it?"

She tilted her head, her big blonde curls barely moving. "Yes, take it you got my name from that tall, dark, detective over there."

She jutted her chin toward someone behind me, though I knew who she meant. I tried not to look to see if Detective Waltz was watching us.

Though I had a feeling he was always watching

me, no matter what I did.

The electricity that traveled down to my toes tried to tell me it was all business from him and not that he had a thing for women covered in dog hair.

I had to fess up. "I did, but only because I didn't get yours at the funeral home. I'm assuming you wouldn't want to head over to the ranch after this and maybe join my friends and I at The Boot and Saddle."

She raised an eyebrow. "The what?"

There was no way to sugar coat the joint and make it seem like a bottle service place in Dallas to which she was accustomed to patronizing. But hey, a drink was a drink.

I forced the biggest smile I could. "It's the local bar in town. Nothing special with a lot of cheap liquor and vinyl seats. But better than you having to deal with Miss Tiffany's glares, I figured."

She stared at me long and hard before finally a small smile crossed her lips. "It's Amber."

"It's what?"

"My name is Amber. And that's exactly the color of liquid I hope they serve at this bar, if we're going."

———

"I can't believe we're going here," Piper hissed from the driver's seat of her fancy black Escalade complete with tan leather seats. "And you asked Haley's friend,"

The car was an anniversary gift from Tad after he spent way too much money in Durant, she claims.

Sophia and I left our cars at the cemetery, since Piper offered and both our cars were covered in dog and kid fur.

"Not friend. Girlfriend. It's Haley's girlfriend," Sophia piped up from the backseat.

"And a possible suspect," I added.

"So, after your little talk with the guy in the fitted suit, you came to that conclusion?" Piper asked. Immediately, I sat up straighter, on high alert.

Sophia patted the back of my seat. "Which by the way, you didn't tell us Mr. Dallas Detective was a hottie. He's better looking than a Detective Stabler and Special Agent Booth all rolled into one delicious package."

My face heated up as I tried to ignore her words.

Though she was right, I wasn't about to admit that to her or anyone.

"What he looks like isn't the point," I said with a touch of attitude. "Let's focus, people. He told me she was questioned this morning. And if she really is a suspect, who better to interrogate her than us...and ply her with whatever alcohol Piper orders."

"You make it sound like all I do is drink," Piper argued, "and if that's the case, I have a handle of vodka at my house that's way better than whatever bottom of the barrel they're shooting at the old B&S." Her hands tightened on the steering wheel as if she took the statement personally.

"Do you really want to bring a possible killer back to your house? To your kids?" I asked.

Piper blinked hard then shook her head. "No. I guess not."

We were all silent for a few beats before Sophia cleared her throat. "Do you really think she did it?"

I shrugged, a nagging feeling at the back of my neck, like I was missing something I couldn't quite put my finger on. "I don't know. The detective seems to think so. I mean he said he questioned her at the station, so it's possible."

"But do you?" Sophia raised her eyebrows.

I sighed, the heat and wariness of the day dragging on, with a dull ache forming in my temple. "I don't know, honestly. It could all be a wild goose chase, but I know someone went after Billy and me for that matter. And if we don't find out who it is, the golf cart might not be the only thing to run me off the course."

A sleek red sports car stood out among the pickup trucks lined up at the Boot and Saddle. that's metal facade blended in with the storage facility that the bar was built into.

Being in the bible belt, Pecan was still a dry county, so the only bar in town, aside from the country club, required a membership to join. That membership was a piece of cardstock you signed and paid a dollar so you could have unlimited drinks.

Most people just went into Dallas for their libations or drank at home instead of dealing with the rules. But a local group that loved to play the old jukebox and drink their Shiners on tap paid their dollar to frequent the Boots and Saddle.

"So, we are guessing that's Amber's car or maybe she drives one of the pickup trucks?" Sophia asked, her eyes running over the length of the car as we pulled in beside it.

"Stop staring it like it's a piece of steak," Piper hissed, and "careful you don't hit it with my doors, either. We don't need to give her a reason to hate us."

Piper hopped out of the car, and Sophia and I gingerly followed, making sure to keep our doors far away from the shiny red paint of the sports car.

A wave of thick smoke curled out as soon as we opened the metal door of the bar.

If the country club was considered the nice bar of Pecan, even with its haphazard ripped vinyl seats, then the Boot and Saddle was at the other end of the spectrum. And that didn't say much about either of them.

With its sticky linoleum floor, mostly burnt-out neon signs, and high top tables, held together with duct tape, it wasn't exactly cream of the crop.

But being the only real bar in Pecan, every duct taped-bar stool was occupied, keeping the leather-clad bartender busy pouring drink after drink. She had the same brassy blonde dye job that I remembered from the last time I had a taste for B&S rotgut, an unfortunate color I was sure came from a bottle and not Mrs. Bev's hands.

I easily spotted the blonde beauty from the funeral home in the middle of the smokey room, but I wasn't expecting the person sitting next to her at the rickety high-top table.

Edgar tipped back his beer bottle to his smiling lips while Amber tossed her hair over her shoulder, laughing as she swirled the liquid in her drink.

"Edgar…hey…" I said cautiously as we approached, Piper and Sophia falling behind me as if somehow, I would protect them. The only weapon I possibly had was one of Bandit's bully sticks in my pockets. That wouldn't take out one, let alone, two people.

Edgar cleared his throat in an attempt to hide his surprise. "Leslie, what are you doing here?" He adjusted his bolo tie with one hand and gripped his beer bottle with the other.

"Um…"

Sophia stepped beside me, crossing her arms over her chest. "We should be asking you the same thing; shouldn't you be at the funeral luncheon? Not talking to a pretty blonde at a bar?"

Edgar chuckled, looking from Amber then back to us, his grip loosening on the bottle as he did so. "You think me and Amber? No, no. This is our lawyer's daughter, and I was just as surprised as you to see her here. Though, I'm sure we have the same feeling about being around Mrs. Tiffany right now."

He took a long pull of his beer and Amber looked down at her glass, scrunching her nose.

"Lawyer's daughter?" Piper asked, suddenly at my side, leaning in like she was trying to get the right station on the radio.

"Well, I guess, since she's joined the firm, she's kind of our lawyer, too. For the Williams estate. Wouldn't ya say so, Amber?" Edgar asked, nudging her elbow.

"Someone has to put up with y'all," she said with a forced laugh before downing her drink.

Well, that was something she could have said at the funeral, but why hide that…unless…

A cold chill crept across the back of my neck and it wasn't from the rickety air conditioning unit.

My flight or fight senses kicked in, and I should have been running for the hills. Yet my feet were cemented to the very spot as I stared at the two biggest suspects for murder.

If they were working together, Amber would have known I was at the country club with one quick text from Edgar. It wouldn't take long after his ranting to make it into Pecan from Dallas without raising suspicion.

Suddenly my stomach dropped, and I racked my brain for any excuse to get out of there.

But leave it to Piper. "We were planning on meeting Amber for a drink before heading to pay our respects, but I guess we can join the both of you," she quickly said, pulling up one of the rickety stools to the table.

I hoped she was packing because she just scooted next to two possible killers when she needed to look for an escape route.

"Why the heck not?" Edgar said," waving us into their circle expansively. "More the merrier, and I'm sure Amber's tired of hearing an old man like me gab anyway." He put his hand on her shoulder as she straightened her spine.

He cleared his throat, and looked at me sideways. "I just didn't know y'all knew each other. Tell me, Leslie, how do you know Rick Rangor's daughter?" He shifted in his seat so that the stool creaked loudly beneath him.

"We just met today, Mr. Williams," Amber quickly replied.

"Yeah, Amber said she was a friend of Haley's, but we didn't know she was the family lawyer, too," I added, my throat going dry as I took a big swallow.

"Oh, yeah, her and Hales go way back." Edgar teared up. "They've been playing together since they were knee high to a pig's eye. Glad my niece gave her a place to stay. I don't blame Haley not wanting to stay with that stepmother of hers. Or in the place my brother..." He swallowed the last of his beer then pounded the bottle on the table.

"Let's get some more drinks, whadda ya say ladies? Next rounds on me," he slurred.

"Oh, I don't think..." Amber started, but Edgar already had his hand up, signaling to the bartender.

"Sadie, get me another Shiner, whatever Amber's having, and three Texas teas for these lovely ladies," he yelled over the twangy country music that started to cringe from the speakers.

"I really don't think..."

Before I could finish my sentence, another noise pierced my ears, alongside the banging of the front door.

"Hey, no dogs in here," Sadie yelled just as I turned to get a giant muddy pawing from Bandit.

"Bandit, what are you doing here?" Of course, he didn't answer my question, just skidded across the floor, his tiny muddy paws making their own little trail.

My heart stopped then started banging wildly before I picked up my little shaking dog, his little muddy footprints all over my mom's dress, but I didn't care. I held her shaking little body against my chest, scratching behind his ears as I tried to control his whimpers.

"That's what I'd like to know, too," a deep voice boomed.

I winced, looking up to see Detective Waltz strolling in.

"Is there a problem, Detective?" Amber asked in a voice that definitely said she had some practice talking to the law.

"Local police called me down from the ranch to see what was going on at the Boot and Saddle, and I found this guy in the parking lot near an SUV with four flat tires." He stood with his hands in his pockets of his suit coat, ever the calm and collected.

Piper leapt up from the stool. "An SUV? MY CAR!"

She high tailed it out of the bar, not even waiting for anyone else to follow or to confirm it was hers.

"How…? Wha…?" I looked around the room, all eyes now on our table.

"Leslie, can we have a word? Outside."

And just like that, my day went from bad, to even worse.

14

Tad, Piper's husband, rolled up in his water department work truck just as the brigade of on lookers and local police gathered around the gravel parking lot.

The lanky man with his dusty cowboy boots and permanent scowl adjusted his Pecan Pirates hat before finally looking at his wife, sobbing on the hood of her prized SUV.

Pushing aside the onlookers, he rushed to her side as she continued to cry about her car, ignoring Sophia and I standing there and a muddy dog shaking in my arms.

"Don't worry, baby. A couple rounds of poker in Durant, and we'll get those tires taken care of in no time," he said with that lazy drawl.

"My carrrrrr. My carrrrrr. Why does this have to happen to me? Whyyyy?" Her crocodile tears piled as she wailed like Nancy Kerrigan.

It was just a car, and I was sure insurance would take care of it.

But to her it was more.

To me, it wasn't just slashed tires though. This had the same chill slinking down my spine as the other night at the golf course. The person who tried to run me over was now going after my friends and possibly my dog.

Looking away from the couple, I bent my head down to bury my face in Bandit's wet fur. I wished at that moment more than anything the dog could really have a conversation with me. How the heck did he make the trip down here? And why?

At least he wasn't hurt. Just a few popped tires and a trip to my neighbor Danny's shop would make them good as new.

But as for my shaking Dashie and my own weak knees, I didn't know if we'd ever be the same.

"What happened to you, little boy?" I whispered into Bandit's floppy ears.

"I'd like to know the same thing," the deep voice boomed, so close that I all but jump back in surprise.

Detective Waltz stood in front of me without the signature smirk I expected, but a deep scowl as he looked from me to my dog.

Bandit curled up in my arms, his little wet nose digging into my chin as his muddy paws kept pawing until he made himself comfortable enough to flop onto his back.

"You're the one who found me sitting with my friends at the bar and saw me at the funeral. Did you happen to see my little dog come after me? After all, if you were the good detective trailing me, you should have seen this," I snapped, probably not the best thing to do to a police officer or when I had a shaking dog in my arms.

Luckily, Bandit didn't seem to be roused and only gave a light snort before burying his furry head in my chest.

Detective Waltz nodded and then said something that surprised me. "I'm sorry."

"You're…wha…?"

I don't think a man had ever said that to me, especially not a detective.

I swallowed hard, trying to focus on what he was saying and not that his words had my insides going all mushy.

"You know what, I need to give Jake a call. Him

and the kids have been texting me nonstop anyway, so I'll have him pick up some Sonic for dinner. I'll leave you two be," Sophia said, clasping my shoulder and giving it a little squeeze before her flip flops crunched on the gravel as she walked away.

I didn't dare look up to see her broad smile as she walked away, instead trying to keep my focus on the detective and will my cheeks not to turn as red as they felt.

He let out a breath, raking his fingers through his brown hair that was starting to get a little long at the sides, curling near his ears. He could probably use a trim, but I wasn't about to offer that grooming advice right now. Not when I wanted to hear what he had to say next.

"I said I'd post up an officer and I didn't. The town was strapped with the funeral and an accident near 1138. If we'd had someone watching you…"

I put my hand up, swallowing the lump in my throat. "I told you I didn't need someone to protect me."

He rubbed the bridge of his nose. "Miss Winters."

"Leslie," I corrected.

The detective sighed. "Leslie."

I nodded slowly, watching the way his shoulders

stiffened as he took in a few shallow breaths in through his nose and out his mouth.

"Someone out there is obviously after you and your friends. I'm going to make sure that an officer is watching your place at all times even if it has to be me."

"You? At my place?" I sputtered, thinking of my mom waddling out in her housecoat to ask him in for chicken fried steak and chat him up about his love life.

He arched an eyebrow, a small smile crossing his lip. "What? You got something to hide?"

"W-w-hat? No? I mean except for the fact that I'm living in my parents' house and sleeping on my old twin bed with my dog."

I clamped my mouth shut.

I could NOT believe I just said that out loud.

Luckily before the good detective could respond, we were interrupted by the bickering of Susan Williams, her husband having the good sense to look sullen, his chin down to his chest as she continued pointing a manicured fingernail at him.

"Is everything okay, Mr. and Mrs. Williams?" Detective Waltz asked, luckily turning away from me so I could get a minute to breathe.

And assess the muddy situation on my dress,

along with little bits of brown fur. Of course, Bandit was already snoozing against my chest, his paws tucked together as his head lolled to the side.

At least someone was comfortable.

Though there was still the question of how he got here.

My parents' house was a few blocks as the crow flies if he ran through the wooded areas, but he'd never done that before. And why would he?

Something had to scare him all right, and I wondered if that something was the same one who flattened Piper's tires and chased me down with the golf cart at the country club.

Whoever this was, was getting closer and closer to my inner circle.

My head and my heart combated at what to do next.

Would this person stop if I stopped looking for him? Or her?

Or would they work even harder to make sure I did stop?

"Edgar, you tell the good detective right now what you told me," Susan commanded, my head snapping up to watch her in response.

With her hands on her hips, the jangling of one million little bracelets moving with her wrists, she looked every bit the eccentric music teacher we'd all had since elementary school. The one no one actually took seriously when she picked up a broom stick and told us to hush.

"Not now, Susie Q," Edgar mumbled, his head still down.

"Is there a problem, Mr. and Mrs. Williams?" Detective Waltz was all business, his arms crossed over his chest, his legs spread in a power stance, like some kind of half-cocked Superman.

A pretty different sight from the music teacher in her big red hair and bright black and white polka dotted dress covering her squat frame like a sack of potatoes. Whoever was giving her funeral fashion advice, or fashion advice in general, should probably be fired.

"Oh, yeah, there's a problem, besides my husband talking to a pretty young thing instead of being at his brother's luncheon," Susan snapped.

Edgar shook his head. "Come on, we both know that I'm not interested in other gals. It's not like that with Amber. She's young enough to be my daughter."

And dating his niece.

But I kept my lips shut, not ready to interrupt whatever they were going to say.

"Well then you can just tell the detective right here what that little Miss Amber had to say."

"Honey, come on…"

Susan cut her eyes so hard at Edgar I swore she was about to slash daggers through him.

I tried not to gulp, standing straighter as if I were the one being reprimanded.

Edgar finally sighed, taking off his Stetson and wiping his sweaty brow. "While we were having a drink, Amber happened to mention she and Billy had a conversation a few nights ago about the property. Apparently, Billy didn't want to deal with Amber as his lawyer, even though she's set to take on more of her daddy's business as he looks toward retirement."

Detective Waltz kept prying, as I've learned he is wont to do. "Any reason he wouldn't want to deal with Amber in particular?"

Edgar shuffled from one foot to the other. "Well…"

"Because she's a homosexual whose defiling our niece," Susan hissed.

Detective Waltz had the good sense to blink but not say a darn thing in response.

Honestly, I was impressed that Susan didn't use a worse slang.

"Now, Susie Q, it wasn't like that. Billy just hadn't come around to the idea of it yet. With it being his only daughter and Amber's daddy being our lawyer since our Pops and Mama were alive."

Edgar may have been saying the words with that "gee golly" type of voice, but there was a hesitation to each word. As if he himself didn't believe in what he was saying.

"So, Mr. Williams and Amber had a disagreement before he passed. Is what you're saying?" Detective Waltz added, one perfect eyebrow arched. Not that I was examining his face too closely or anything.

"No," Edgar practically bellowed at the same time Susan nodded and mouthed, "Yes."

Detective Waltz rubbed the bridge of his nose then swiped his thumb across his forehead before nodding. "Okay, it looks like I will have a few more questions for Miss Rangor. Don't worry. We will get this settled as soon as possible."

With a few more niceties and a pat on the back from the detective, Susan and Edgar went back toward their car.

I thought I could easily slink away, too, maybe get a ride with Sophia, Jake, and the kids to my car, but before I could even turn, Detective Waltz's voice boomed loud enough to have Bandit stirring.

"And where do you think you're going, Leslie?"

I blinked hard, turning toward him with a small shrug off my shoulders. "Um, hoping to get a ride home from Sophia and grab my car at the funeral home. Maybe check the fence to see how Bandit ended up getting all the way over here and through my parents back gate once I get home?"

"Why don't I give you a ride to the funeral home and then I can check that fence myself?" he asked, his words to the point, yet my heart stammered with each little phrase.

"Uh…well…you don't need to do that."

Then there went that dang smile of his. "I insist, Leslie."

And who was I to say no to a man of the law when he was offering?

Especially since I wasn't sure what would be waiting at home.

15

I assumed big city detectives had a lot of money.

Maybe I was misinformed by a bunch of cop shows or maybe the good Detective Waltz was a humble guy and just preferred to have an older Suburban with a little duct tape on the seats and ash trays still in the door handles, filled with Jolly Rancher wrappers like my Mee Maw used to have.

"You know it's really no problem for me to call my mom, especially since I've got Bandit," I said again, buckling the seat belt around us. Bandit perched on my lap, his nose in the air smelling every little bit of fast food and coffee stench he could find.

"Really, Leslie, it's no trouble, and I really do want to take a look around your house. Make sure nobody's lurking," he said, starting up the car that was more of a sputter than the purr of newer models.

The looky-loos gathered around the parking lot had started to disperse while a few of the local cops hovered near their own respective vehicles. This would surely be the talk of the luncheon if it were even still going on at this point.

Sighing, I wondered how soon Tiffany Williams would get word of this. Would I even have a job as a dog groomer anymore if she knew the trouble I was getting into. Heck, would anyone hire me if word of my troubles got out?

I glanced over at the man driving, his jaw clenched as he maneuvered through the gravel parking lot and onto the street.

"So, since you're being so chummy, calling me Leslie, and giving me rides, does this mean I get to use your first name too? Or should I keep calling you Detective Waltz?" I asked, finding a heat rising to my cheeks even as I asked the simple question.

At least talking to the detective would have me thinking about my business and not the other pressing fact of a killer on the loose.

I would be safe with the man with a handgun pressed against his trousers, right?

At least I hoped it would.

Adam swallowed hard before a small smile appeared on his face that had me smiling in return. "You can call me Adam. Just not in front of the boys in blue, okay? Wouldn't want them thinking I'm giving you preferential treatment."

"But you kind of are, aren't you? I mean you're giving me a ride home. Not questioning me as if I'm a suspect." I gulped, my eyes suddenly feeling like they were about to pop out of my head. "Which I'm not, right?"

He laughed, shaking his head as my shoulders lightened, the tension in them finally releasing as I let out a breath.

"No, I wouldn't be riding in the car with you right now alone if you were."

"Well, we aren't alone, technically," I said almost too quickly as I ran my hand down the length of my dog's coarse coat. "We have Bandit, here."

My dog turned and licked my chin in response to hearing his name, and I rewarded him with a good scratch behind his ears; he snorted in response.

"As good of a guard dog as I think you have there, not enough to keep you out of trouble."

Detective Waltz glanced at me out of the corner of his eye before running his thumb down Bandit's nose.

Bandit had the nerve to paw at him and lick his hand, the little traitor.

"Hey, not my fault someone did that. You have to know none of that was me, right? And it couldn't be Amber or Edgar if they were with me. Unless they have accomplices…" My voice trailed off as I faced the detective.

My original suspect was Edgar, and Adam had said he was questioning Amber. If they were working together, neither one of them could have deflated the tires on Piper's car or let Bandit loose.

So, …who else was there?

The detective sighed, shaking his head. "I think you're overreaching on a lot of stuff here, Leslie."

"Well *ADAM,* then where should I be reaching or not reaching?" I huffed, crossing my arms over my chest. Bandit snorted, looking first at Adam and then me before resting his head on the console between us.

The detective had the audacity to laugh. "Did you just call me by my first name finally instead of just Detective Waltz?"

I let out a deep breath, blowing my bangs out of

my eyes, feeling a blush cross my face so I turned toward the window, pulling my arms tighter around me. "Well, it's your name isn't it? And if you're going to call me Leslie and tell me I'm reaching, figure I could call you Adam."

He didn't say anything, the silence passing between us like thick molasses in the winter.

It stayed that way until we got to the funeral home.

I knew I needed to thank him for the ride, as my good southern manners always dictated, but right now I wanted to get far away from the man.

So I just offered a smile and a wave as I got in my car, Bandit close at my side.

Turning on my vehicle and backing out of the parking spot, a little worry prickled at the back of my neck.

Slowly I glanced in the rearview mirror before putting my car into drive and heading down Main.

The black SUV was a constant shadow at my back which should have been comforting but also left a chill in the muggy air of my vehicle.

It stayed there all the way past main street and as we turned down the gravel road leading toward my house.

As soon as I rounded the bend by the side of Mom's prized magnolia tree and the old metal workshop shop came into view, my fears were founded.

"Wha…."

I pulled my car to a halt and Adam stopped short of the circle drive, barely missing a set of combs and brushes strewn around the gravel.

Not only were my dog combs and brushes all over the drive, but my hoses, clippers, and even some of my Pop's old tools had been thrown out of the open door of the shop.

Adam shot out of his car, already at my window with his hand on his holster.

"Stay here," he commanded.

Bandit whined in my arms as soon as he saw Adam's face but had the good sense to stay in my arms, his eyes on the window.

Adam's gun was now in his hands, held straight out as he approached the shop.

My heart stopped beating almost entirely as every hair on the back of my arms and neck stood on end.

I held my breath, waiting for what would pop out next.

"This is Detective Adam Waltz with Dallas PD.

Come out," he shouted, still a few yards away from the shop.

Nothing moved or answered in return as I tried to control my heart and my lungs, but both seized up, watching the detective circling the little metal shop.

He slowly pulled out a walkie talkie from his side. "This is Detective Adam Walsh. I'm at the Winters' residence in Pecan, requesting back up immediately."

Something came back over the speakers but I couldn't hear it through the car. I could barely hear anything but Adam's voice, my rapidly beating heart, and Bandit, the great guard dog who decided now was a time to take a nap and snore loudly against my chest.

My heart pounded, my throat going dry as I waited for something to move in the shop. Or for the detective to do something.

What if no back up came and there was a vengeful murderer in the shop, coming out with guns blazing, and my best shears in his hand?

Nothing moved. Not even the detective, standing there with his gun still drawn, slowly inching toward the shop.

"Bandit, should we do something," I whispered.

Bandit snorted before stirring in my arms. Then he opened his big beady eyes, blinking slowly. He must have heard the brush of wind or something. His ears perked up and he sat bolt upright before barking at the window.

Adam's head snapped in my direction, glaring, before he looked back at the shop then to Bandit, now perched in the window, barking his little head off.

"Detective Waltz, Dallas PD, I'm armed and I urge you to come out with your hands up," he yelled, his voice barely audible over Bandit's shrill barks.

"Bandit, hush," I hissed, trying to grab at his little chest and paws and pull him off the dash.

But Bandit was quicker, dodging left and scampering over the console and driver's seat until he could roll down the passenger's side window.

"BANDIT, NO," I gasped, frantically fumbling my arms but getting pulled back by the seatbelt as I watched my little ten-pound Dashie bound out of the window, barking his head off as he ran past Detective Waltz.

"BANDIT," I yelled, undoing my seatbelt, and scrambling out the door before I could think better of it.

My shoes crunched against the gravel, my footing nearly giving out with each step against the cheap plastic dress shoes I'd found at the back of my closet from high school.

"Leslie," Adam's voice was already a distant fade behind me as I bolted after Bandit, catching him just as his little paws stopped in the entrance of the shop.

Or what was my shop.

The twelve-by-twelve metal building had gone from the quaint little room that I'd decorated with my own painted murals of bathing Dashies and little dog beds that resembled the spa chairs of my old salon, to something I didn't recognize.

All of the little pink chairs were ripped and turned over, along with the bath and dryer, laying along an array of colored brushes and water seeping through the wooden floor.

"My…Stars…" I managed to breathe, covering my mouth.

Adam quickly followed, his gun still out as he paced around me, shouting something about being an armed detective and looking under each overturned object.

Adam barked directions into his walkie talkie "The building is clear, but still requesting back up."

The staticky voice came over his walkie talkie, but I wasn't listening.

I was just staring at all I'd built, now just spread all over the floor like it was nothing.

Tears pricked my eyes as I tried to survey all of the damage.

"Bandit, no." I managed to get out of my stupor long enough to grab Bandit before he started licking up some fallen cleaning solution from the brush bottle.

The red and blue lights of the local PD flashed behind me.

Adam must have said something as he led me back out of the shop, but all I could do was grab Bandit, pulling him to my chest and burying my face in his fur.

How could someone do this?

Why would they do this?

A sob caught in my chest as tears fully streamed down my cheeks, along with my cheap clearance mascara that was supposed to be waterproof but fell in big globs down my face.

Everything I worked so hard for, now laying across the driveway.

All of it gone.

Someone was after me.

This was more than just a warning now.

This was telling me to watch my back.

"Leslie? Leslie. Hey, look at me." Adam's usually gruff voice had softened as I slowly turned to meet his gaze.

At least he had the good sense not to smile or frown. His face still as he cleared his throat. "The officers just informed me they found a pair of hair clippers, covered in dog fur at the Boot and Saddle. Ones they'd like you to identify."

My breath caught in my throat as I slowly shook my head. "I…I didn't bring those there. You have to believe me."

He nodded, swallowing hard. "I do, Leslie. I believe your whereabouts and that you wouldn't take those to your friend's car, but someone did and I think that someone is trying to send you a warning."

"A…a…warning? But Detective…I…"

Words failed me as I pulled Bandit closer, wishing somehow, I could just disappear into his fur instead of the chaos around me.

The detective held his hand up to his chest, his palms out toward me.

"Look, I botched the job the first time I tried to protect you, and I'm not going to let that happen again. I'll be posting up with my car outside of your house. When I can't be here, we'll have another uniformed officer on assignment. Whoever did this, has it out for you, Leslie, and you have my word that we're going to find them."

"Adam…you don't need to do that," I pressed, but even as I said the words, I couldn't keep the trembling out of my voice.

He took a step closer, the fronts of his now dusty loafers brushing up against my shoes. "I do, Leslie. It's my job."

16

By the time Ma and Dad came back from the luncheon at the ranch, the gossip mill was already in full swing.

I thought maybe they'd be so concerned about their daughter's wellbeing that they wouldn't notice the cop cars or the certain handsome detective still standing next to me, cuddling Bandit.

Dang that traitor.

Ma fluttered out of Dad's rusty pick-up truck, barreling toward me like a woman on a mission.

Instead of her usual floral house dress, she'd donned a black, long sleeve wrapped dress. Mrs. Bev must have worked overtime before the luncheon because she had tamed Mom's hair into a bun with so much hairspray that it defied the Texas heat.

Guess that explained why I didn't see my parents at the funeral; they were too busy waiting for Ma to get her hair done.

I didn't even get to stop and say a word to my dad sauntering out of the car with his black Stetson low over his forehead. Instead, it was Ma that came to an abrupt stop in front of me.

"Leslie, all this work to bring a man home?" She fluttered her eyelashes, and I couldn't tell if she was trying to embarrass me or REALLY embarrass me.

"Mom…" I started but Adam cut me off with his free hand, the other wrapped around my traitorous Bandit who had curled up in the crook of his arm like a prized chicken.

"Mrs. Winter, I'm Detective Adam Waltz, with Dallas PD. We met the other night at the golf course." He was all business with his firm handshake but Ma had turned into a giggling girl.

"Of course, I remember. I wasn't expecting to see you again. Why, it was the talk at the ranch that the handsome, young detective gave my daughter a ride home from the Boot and Saddle."

"Ma," I said through gritted teeth.

Now was not the time to try and play matchmaker.

Especially when the contents of my shop were strewn across the driveway and all of the looky-loo neighbors had to have the gossip mill texting tree going.

"You know detective, Mrs. Bev, the local hairdresser? She was so busy today that my dear husband and I barely made the end of the graveside service. Well, anyway, she was talking to Danny down the way, and he said that he saw someone rooting around in the shop, and I thought 'Well, Leslie isn't supposed to be working. She said she was going with the girls for a drink', then I remembered the detective and..."

I put my hand out, stopping Ma before she said any more about Adam. "Danny saw someone rooting around in the shop? When was that?"

My heart thudded as I looked wide-eyed from Ma back to the detective.

She put her hands on her hips. "Why I don't know, Les. Sometime after we left the cemetery, I guess. You know, Danny didn't make it to the funeral on a count of the last one he went to was his mama's, but he couldn't miss a free buffet."

Ma took out her portable fan, blowing it against

her face as she kept talking. "Anyway, I was just enjoying Mrs. Bev's deviled eggs when I heard her talking to Danny, who we all know didn't come to the funeral but wouldn't miss anyone's funeral potatoes at a luncheon."

Ma scratched her head then nodded. "I think it was a little bit after Susan made a big show of having to go pick Edgar up when she heard he was having a drink with their lawyer at the Boot and Saddle."

"Ma'am, do you mind if we could discuss this further, maybe nail down a few exact times?" Adam asked. He cleared his throat, and I swore his cheeks were tinged redder than a tomato.

"Are you trying to ask me if you can court my daughter?" Ma raised her eyebrows high in her head. If Adam wasn't already blushing, his face was on fire by now.

Not the time, Ma. Not the time.

He cleared his throat, and not even glancing in my direction, Adam handed Bandit off to me.

My little guard dog protested with a whine as I pulled him close, but from the way he snuggled against my chest, I think all the barking had tired him out.

"Uh, let's take a step aside here for a few

moments, Mrs. Winter," Adam said gently to Ma, more cordial I thought than she deserved.

"Whatever you say, Detective." Ma shot a wink over her shoulder before following him a few steps away. He quickly pulled out his notebook and cleared his throat, ready to get down to . business. But by the flapping of Ma's hands, I had a feeling she wasn't talking about the case.

"Y'all right, Les?" Dad's calloused hand was on my shoulder, and I let out a sigh of relief I didn't realize I'd been holding in.

From the moment I first set foot in Pecan, Texas, things had been a whirlwind.

Just when I thought I might be getting my life together, a murderer showed up in our little town.

A sinking feeling hit the pit of my stomach.

The murderer was now after me.

"I don't know, Dad. Honestly."

Running my fingers through Bandit's short coat, I tried to focus on anything instead of the business I'd built up the past few months, now strewn around my parent's gravel drive.

My dear dad read the look of despair on my face. "They're just things, honey. Things can easily be replaced, but you can't." Dad pulled me tighter against him, the warmth of his body radiating off him like a space heater.

Things.

Things I spent what little money I had on.

I was still living at my parents.

And now everything I thought I'd built up was destroyed.

My shoulders shook as I tried to hold back the sob bubbling in my chest.

But it could have been worse.

It could have been me on the gravel instead of my shears and dog shampoo.

"I just heard that detective is going to keep watch out here tonight." Dad's grip tightened on my shoulder.

I nodded, my mouth going dry.

"They're gonna catch whoever did this. The gossip mill runs strong in Pecan and so does neighborhood watch. Whoever it was that broke in here was just lucky your daddy wasn't on the front porch, cleaning his shot gun."

"Dad…" I managed to croak.

He stifled a grin. "I'm just playing. We've had enough violence around here. I just hope that Dallas detective knows what he's doing and all of this trouble leaves Pecan soon."

"You're not the only one…"

———

Dinner with my parents was…well like how dinner with my parents usually was.

Filled with way too much food and a dog begging at my feet.

But it was even more awkward than the usual conversation now that just about fifty yards away, we had a detective posted near our little brick mail box in his black SUV.

"Leslie, are you going to keep staring at the man through the window or do you want to put some chicken on a plate and walk it out there for him?" Ma asked, the smile evident on her lips even before I snapped my gaze back to her.

"What? No," I said quickly, trying to shovel some mashed potatoes in my mouth so I'd stop myself from saying something worse.

Ma didn't say another word, just grabbed a spare plate and loaded it up with okra, chicken, and mashed potatoes then covered it in foil.

She thrust it toward me, raising her eyebrows.

"You saying I need to leave and packing me some food to go?"

"I'm saying, I know you've been snooping around town with Sophia and Piper. So why not bring some food to the man who is doing his own investigating with years of training. And may have saved your hide today?"

Well, guess I couldn't argue with that logic. No matter how much Dad cut his eyes at Ma from across the table, we both knew he wasn't going to say anything.

And, as much as I tried to protest, I knew it wouldn't hurt to get some answers from the detective about who would want to hurt Mr. Williams and now possibly me.

Stepping out into the muggy night air, I swatted away a few mosquitos before shutting the screen door behind me.

My flip flops flopped against the wooden deck, louder with each step down the gravel path toward the parked SUV.

The closer I got to the car, the more my stomach dropped.

What the heck was I going to say to the detective…Adam…right, Adam?

Did he care that I changed out of my black dress and into some leggings and a Dallas Mavericks t-shirt, my hair now twisted into its usual high bun.

Wait, why did I care what he thought of what I was wearing?

I was there to be friendly…and to try and find out just how scared I should be of a killer who was possible after me.

Knocking on the window of the detective's vehicle, I heard the mumbled voices of some kind of radio talk show pouring out of the speakers.

For a trained detective, the man sure did jump when I disturbed his reverie. His head banged so hard against the back of the seat, I let out a yelp of my own, almost knocking the plate of food against my chest.

He rolled down the window, letting out a deep breath. "Leslie? You shouldn't sneak up on a guy like that."

"Shouldn't you be watching the house? Isn't that what you're out here for Mr. Detective?" I raised my eyebrows, putting my free hand on my hip.

He nodded. "All right, you got me there. And what's with the detective stuff? Thought we were on a first name basis, Leslie?"

I looked down, trying to keep the heat from

flushing my cheeks. "Well, figured you were on official business."

I took a chance, looking back up at him as he shook his head, looking out the front window into the neighbor's yard, not that he could see past the variety of cars in various states of repair that Danny had back there.

"Been pretty quiet out here. Not used to the lack of noise."

I nodded in return. "Yeah…peaceful, isn't it?"

He smirked. "Hopefully, it stays that way."

He raised an eyebrow, eying me over the window. "Unless you're about to do something drastic with that plate."

My shoulders shook as I offered the plate to him, almost forgetting the reason I'd come out. "Oh, my ma wanted me to bring you out some dinner."

I could see his face light up even though dusk was falling. "Oh, that's mighty kind. She didn't need to do it." He may have been saying the words, but he'd already lowered the window to reaching for the plate and was unwrapping the foil before I could even finish the sentence.

"Man, this smells good. Did you cook this?"

I snorted. "No, I didn't get that gene."

He shoveled some okra into his mouth, using the plastic cutlery Ma packed with it. His head rolled back against the seat in response. "Dang, that's too bad. I don't think I've had okra this good in, well, ever."

"You mean you don't live near your mama to bring you some Texas home cooking?"

"No. My parents both passed away years ago."

Bless it.

My shoulder sagged as I looked at the detective in a new light.

The hard guy who took care of me.

Were they the reason he became a detective? His parents?

No, now was not the time for being nosey.

I traced a line in the gravel with my toe. "Sorry."

"No need to be sorry. It's not your fault they were drinking and driving. Guess I owe it to them that I became a detective, though. Knew I didn't want to go down the same path they did."

"Wow...that's..." I couldn't even finish my sentence as I watched the moon reflect off his sandy brown hair.

"Heavy, I know. You get used to it in this business. Though, out of all the cases I've worked on,

I've never met a woman as stubborn, but then makes up for it by bringing me home cooking."

Adam smiled, and I had to look away to bite back my own grin. "No need to call me names."

"Aw, you think I'm picking on ya? Sorry, just calling it like I see it. You seem to be the type of woman that won't take no for an answer. Even after people in authority tell you not to do something, you still go for it."

"One might call that loyalty or persistence. Not stubbornness."

I held my head up, taking in a deep breath as I put my fists on my hips like a Wonder Woman power pose.

He nodded, thoughtfully chewing his food. "Okay. I'll give you that one. But whatever you want to call it, you do need to be careful. I really don't want to see anything happen to you if this person is after you."

I put my hand to my chest and let out an exaggerated sigh. "Aw, why Mr. Adam do you care about me?"

He swallowed hard, the silence sitting between us as our eyes met in the moon light.

But before he could respond, a dash of brown fur darted up my legs, climbing until Bandit was in my arms and lurching his paws in through the window just in time to grab a piece of chicken before Adam could pull it away.

"Bandit!" I hushed, pulling the happy gobbling pup back from the window.

"It's okay," Adam said laughing. "He probably deserves a piece with all the work he's done."

My face heated as I held onto the little dog. "Well, um, we should go now that you have your food, but hopefully you're watching the house better than your food."

"I am, Leslie. I promise."

I didn't let another silence rise up between us as I put my head down, walking Bandit toward the house.

"You know, your mama was having a moment there, Bandit? I don't know if that was a good or bad thing you interrupted," I whispered to him.

He gave me a lick on the nose in response.

"Yeah. Probably a good thing."

Even though I found myself glancing out my bedroom window all night. Either worried the detective wasn't watching hard enough or maybe I was just watching him.

17

My phone buzzed for the millionth time from my side table, rattling the miscellaneous cups I needed to take to the kitchen.

I groaned, covering my eyes with my arm. The free one that is, Bandit had my other arm pinned, sprawled over me as he was with his head on the pillow, snoozing away like he didn't have a care in the world.

Which he didn't.

He wasn't the one probably getting another text that someone wanted to cancel or 'reschedule' their grooming appointment.

Apparently, word does get around fast in Pecan, and no one wanted their dog groomed by someone with a possible killer after them.

"I don't want to hear any more excuses," I muttered, reaching my hand out to grasp for the phone lost somewhere between my books and random pieces of scratch paper I wrote notes on, a few of the glasses clinking with it.

Buzz.

Buzz.

BUZZZZZZZZZZZZZZZZ.

My phone vibrated against the nightstand, moving along like one of those little wind-up operated chicks they used to give out in Easter baskets.

That finally woke Bandit up as he lifted his head, snorting right into my open mouth as I yawned.

"Dang it, fine." I swung my arm onto the whicker surface, slapping my palm over the phone before sliding it unlocked to my ear.

"Yes, I know there might be a potential murderer after me and my shop was overturned. You don't have to make up other excuses for not wanting to bring your dog to be groomed," I spat, my voice still groggy in its morning fog.

"Well, hello to you too, Miss Sunshine," Sophia sang from the other end.

"Why are you calling? Why not just text like a normal person?" I groaned slowly sitting up, my joints popping as I pushed the glaring Bandit to his side of the pillow.

He curled his upper lip in a sneer, looking down at my hands like I had the audacity to wake him up.

For a little thing, he sure could take up a lot of room. And have enough of an attitude for a much bigger dog.

"I did, and you didn't answer. I almost had to drive over to your house, but rumor has it there's still a detective's car parked outside. Does your mom know? If you're trying to have a hook up, I'm all for it, but really, in your parents' house?"

I sighed, rubbing the bridge of my nose.

Guess I should have told Sophia before the rumor mill got to her.

Recapping everything that happened when Adam and I pulled up, I paused for Sophia's usual "HOLY HECK" responses until I got everything was out. Including the awkward moment outside that Bandit interrupted and all these early morning texts.

"Well, I'll be over in about fifteen with coffee before you drive me to Harry Hines."

I bolted straight up in bed. "What?"

"I need to get some supplies down on Harry Hines Street, and I don't want to drive Dallas traffic by myself, so you're gonna come with me to help me merge. Did I mention there was coffee?"

I rubbed my temple, a dull ache forming in my already sleepy head. "You're going to need to learn to drive Dallas by yourself one of these days. What if I'm busy?"

She huffed. "You literally just said your clients have been canceling on you."

"There is the whole someone killed a man in Pecan and may be after me thing…"

"Don't worry, I have a plan for that."

My heart thudded. "A plan?" I loved Sophia, but sometimes her plans could get me in trouble.

She laughed. "Don't worry. Just get dressed and I'll be there in ten. Or fifteen. Or however long it takes my mother-in-law to get here and how long the line is at the coffee shop. The one where the lady is always spouting conspiracy theories. She may be a little crazy, but she makes the best caramel macchiatos."

I sighed. "Okay, fine. Get mine with a cronut and make sure she doesn't try and sell you on any more of those random meetings she's always attending."

"Will do."

We hung up the call, and I quickly hopped in

the shower, trying to rinse away all of the craziness of the day before.

Sophia was never early or, on time for that matter, so it didn't matter that I took a longer shower than usual or did my hair before putting on a clean pair of jeans and a tank top. Okay, and maybe a little more makeup than I usually would in case Adam was still parked outside.

Swiping my bangs to the side before pulling my hair into a high bun, I took another look in the mirror.

Sure, a lot had happened this past week, but why was it showing on my face all of a sudden?

Were the dark circles under my eyes somehow even darker?

Or was this just how I always looked.

"Really, Les, is this what you're worried about?" I muttered to myself before swiping another coat of concealer under my eyes. Then I grabbed my phone.

Bandit eyed me from his bed perched by the fireplace.

"I'm only going to be gone for a bit, okay, boy?"

He sat bolt upright, his beady black eyes watching me walk all the way to the door.

"I promise, I'll be back soon. Come on don't

give me that look." I paused with my hand on the door. "Ma left your food out, so don't be begging for second breakfast."

He whined, putting a paw up for a shake.

I wondered how Sophia would feel if I brought him along with for the ride...

Shaking the thoughts out of my head as quickly as they came into my head, I took one last look at my Dashie. "I promise, I'll be back soon, okay?"

I glanced over my shoulder, Bandit's little face peering out of the locked doggy door.

I could take the little dog anywhere in Pecan, but Dallas was no place for a pup.

Maybe I could just ask the nice detective to watch him while I was gone.

Yeah.

That made a good conversation starter.

Somehow, Dad and Ma had gotten out of the house without my hearing them, but as soon as I stepped on the front porch, Adam's window rolled down, and he eyed me over the holly bushes.

His gaze followed me the entire way across the grass as I walked to his car.

I leaned over the side window, the overwhelming smell of coffee and fast food wafting out.

Did he get delivery or was that all from the night before?

"Mornin', didn't expect you to still be here," I said as politely as I could.

"Told ya I would be."

I bit down on my bottom lip, trying to control the little smile blooming against my wishes. "Anything new to report?" I asked, hoping he didn't hear my heart thumping against my chest.

"Well, I think the neighbor's dogs made a baby at around two this morning. The cats, too."

I raised an eyebrow, glancing at the neighbor's chain link fence where her two scrappy hound dogs sprawled on the back cement patio. "Landry and Aikman fighting for dominance again, I reckon. Though I don't think either can have babies, on account of they're both fixed hunting dogs."

Adam had the good sense to flush as he nodded. "Oh. Well, that was the only thing to report. Luckily. And I guess I'd better get to know the difference in female and male dogs."

"I mean, pretty easy if you know where to look."

My cheeks burned as he gave me that dark stare. Why did I even say embarrassing things like that?

I cleared my throat.

"Well, Sophia and I are heading to Dallas today while you watch the house."

He practically choked on his own spit, coughing, and patting his chest. "Are you kidding me, Leslie? Do you not remember what's happened the last twenty-four hours?"

"We are just going down to Harry Hines to get some vinyl. You'll be watching the house, right?" I asked, batting my eyelashes.

Before he could sputter a response through his narrowed face, Sophia's Suburban came barreling down the hill, stopping just short of the driveway.

Sophia held her arm out the window, waving as a musical soundtrack blared through the speakers.

I didn't say anything as I pushed off Adam's car and headed toward Sophia.

But when I heard the sound of the door slamming behind me, it took everything I had not to jump.

"Detective, keeping good watch?" Sophia asked, shooting me a knowing smile as I approached the passenger side of her vehicle, the detective at her window.

"I was just telling Leslie, I don't think it's a great idea for you two to be heading into Dallas right now." He may have been talking to my friend, but his glare was on me as I hopped into the passenger seat.

"Oh, don't worry. I've got protection." She grabbed her purse from the back then pulled out a pink plastic rectangle about six inches long and half an inch thick.

"What is that?" I gasped.

"Taser," she said as if she were just telling me the most normal thing in the world.

"Where did you get that? Is that even legal?" I whispered the last part, glancing at Adam who had the good sense to at least attempt to hide his smile with his hand.

She huffed. "I got it on Amazon Prime this morning, so it has to be, right?"

Adam sighed, shaking his head as he ran his hand down his face.

The dark circles were more prominent around his eyes, along with a days' worth of stubble grazing his cheeks. "Are you two yanking my chain?"

He had to be tired.

Heck, I was tired, and I wasn't the one sitting up all night watching a house and two dogs canoodling.

Sophia shook her head. "No, sir. We just need to

head to Harry Hines for some crafting supplies, and I hate driving Dallas so Leslie is going to help me. Unless you want to ride along? I'm sure we can get you an extra cup of coffee."

She held up her extra-large iced coffee that I knew always had added bits of espresso and caramel.

Luckily, my normal caramel macchiato sat in the cup holder next to hers. I took an extra-long sip, waiting for Adam to reply.

"I'll be here watching the house, but if anything happens, y'all call my number, okay." He pulled a card out of his pocket and handed it to Sophia. Though his steel gaze was locked on me.

My heart thudded heart against my chest.

What was that look for?

Did he know something I didn't? Would he just follow us?

Should I be more worried than I was?

"That has my direct cell phone number," he said with a nod.

"Okayyyy, thank you for your service, sir. And don't worry, I'll get her back in one piece, if Dallas traffic doesn't kill us." Sophia gave him a big toothy grin before downing a big gulp of her drink.

"Stay safe, Leslie," he muttered before tapping on the car door then heading back to his SUV.

What did that freaking mean?

My mind was going a mile a minute as I tried to figure out each little movement.

"Well, now you've got the mister's private number and some coffee. Ya ready?" Sophia asked, revving up the engine as the musical theme's chorus crooned over the stereo.

"Ready as I'll ever be, I guess to fight some middle-aged moms over vinyl," I muttered, still trying to figure out what was hidden behind the detective's words.

Sophia snorted, waiting until we had turned around before she shook her head and revealed her plan. "We aren't actually heading to Harry Hines."

A cold chill crept down my neck. "What?"

"That was the only way I knew to get Mr. Detective off our trail, under the guise of getting you out of the house to a safe location."

"Sophia…You could have told me that's where we were going…" That nagging feeling at my brain now went into full-on overdrive, my heart racing as I tried to mentally come up with what Sophia was going to say before she spoke.

"Yeah, but then you might have said no."

"You're probably right about that."

She blew a raspberry. "Look, just a little drive by on the way to the vinyl store. So, we can still get some crafts, but if we see a certain blonde lawyer and her girlfriend hanging outside the law office near the Galleria, then…"

"Sophia…" My words trailed, the slurp of coffee in my stomach now threatening to gurgle up to my mouth.

"What? You have a better idea about how to solve this mystery? Or do you just want the detective hanging outside your house a little longer?"

I raised an eyebrow, but she didn't even glance in my direction.

This wasn't about some sort of romance with the man in the suit outside of my house. This could put us directly into danger. Snooping and asking questions of the local gossip was one thing, but that was all before someone came for my house.

Now all I could think about was how close this person had come to me. How very real this killer was.

"Come on," she said, full of confidence. "I binge-watched a Netflix special last night and have the perfect plan."

I didn't believe anything good came from a

binge watch. Sophia and I had many of those with Unsolved Mysteries since we were in high school. Usually we just ended up with a headache the next day and looking over our shoulder for masked men.

But Sopha was already on the highway and there was nothing I could say, short of maybe throwing up my coffee to get her to turn around.

I guess at least we had good drinks and a discount taser.

Hopefully, that would be enough.

———

The Rangor law offices looked like every other stucco building in the strip mall. If it weren't for the large black sign announcing the name of the firm, I wouldn't have been able to tell it apart from the cell phone store or the Chinese restaurant.

Sophia parked behind a family's minivan, complete with enough of those stick figure family characters to wonder how they fit them all in one vehicle. We had a full view of the door to Rangor's building,

"So, what's the plan now?" I asked, turning around in my seat to glance around the parking lot.

Sophia nodded, I guess to let me know she'd

heard my question, all the while procuring a Dr. Pepper and some peanuts from her bag.

"Okay, so on this show," adding, "the one I binged?" as if I'd forgotten, "the people sat outside the office until the lawyer went to lunch. Then they followed the lawyer and cornered her by sitting a booth and questioning her until she finally broke."

I blinked hard, realizing now chugging my coffee was a super bad idea as it gurgled in my stomach. "Seriously? That's your plan?"

Sophia shrugged. "You have a better one?"

Before I could respond, a knock came at the window, the force of it jerking my shoulders, the coffee in my stomach now sloshing around and forcing its way to a rumble my stomach.

Slowly I turned to meet the frowning face of Haley Williams herself.

My shoulders relaxed as I rolled down the window, letting out a deep breath. "Haley, what are you doing here…? Visiting the lawyer for lunch?"

She rolled her eyes with a huff. "Amber texted me that she caught a suburban with a Pecan Bull Dogs sticker on the back window. She thought it was my aunt or Tiffany trying to come by again, but I never expected to see you two."

"Why would your aunt and Tiffany be here?" Sophia asked all too eagerly.

"First, why are you two here?" Haley demanded, crossing her arms over her sweater. The same A&M sweater she'd worn the day we found her dad.

A trickle of sweat beaded at the back of my neck.

This wasn't just some Netflix TV show.

This girl had lost her dad.

A lot of her family was pissed.

And I'm sure we weren't helping.

"Look…Haley."

She held up her hand to stop me. "If you're just going to give me some off the cuff, made up answer, save it. I get it, Leslie, you were there when it happened, but whatever is going on with you trying to play amateur detective, it needs to stop, okay? For all of our sakes, just let it be."

I swallowed hard trying to think of the right words.

"I'm sorry," was all I could croak.

"Do you really want to help?" She put her hands on her hips, and I found a little bit of sunshine spurring in my chest but quickly tampered it down.

"Yes?"

"My aunt has been begging me to come help her with her roots. I think it's just an excuse to talk to me, but since you're a dog groomer at all, maybe you can give her some help with her hair?"

I shook my head in a modified double-take. "Didn't she just go to Mrs. Bev?"

Haley shrugged. "I don't know. I thought so, but she seems insistent."

"I don't want to step on any toes…" I muttered.

"Fine. What if I agree to go with you? Y'all can give me a ride there and back here later? Then you can ask me all the questions you're probably dying to, and frame my girlfriend for going after my dad."

"I didn't…I…" I fumbled for the right words.

Sophia beamed from the driver's seat. "Hop on in. Want a Dr. Pepper?"

18

Why Sophia thought this was a good idea, I had absolutely no clue.

But she continued asking Haley questions that really didn't give any answers.

Was she with Amber at the time her dad was killed?

Yes, all day.

Did her and her dad and Tiffany have a fight about Amber?

Yes, they did.

But while Sophia was asking the questions, something else was going through my brain.

The day I found Mr. Williams...

When Susan showed up, she said she was late because she had to see Mrs. Bev.

So why would she need her roots done today, less than two weeks later?

I had a hunch…

Pulling out my phone, I sent a quick text to Mrs. Bev.

Leslie: Hey Mrs. Bev, I normally would do this myself but do you have any openings for next Wednesday night? Maybe around five? Just a quick trim.

Mrs. Bev: Sorry, Leslie, I'd love to help you out, but I close early for Bunco on Wednesdays and all filled up. How about Thursday?

I froze, that very text leaving a nagging feeling in the back of my head.

What was Susan doing if she wasn't with Mrs. Bev?

There was no way I was letting Haley see her aunt alone.

I just wished if I was going into the Lion's Den, I had back up.

Or I could have been wrong about all of this.

Maybe it was just a crazy hunch like I had about Amber and even Edgar.

I let out a deep breath I didn't realize I was holding in.

Maybe I was acting crazy?

I glanced in the backseat at Haley, chatting away without a care in the world.

Like she didn't just see her daddy buried.

What did I really know that could help her?

I had two years of beauty school and a lot of time watching crime shows, but none of that was going to help me.

I reached for my phone to maybe give a heads up to the detective, then I realized Sophia had his card and I hadn't saved his number in my phone.

Was there a way to get to Sophia's wallet without her noticing?

And what the heck would he even say if I texted him?

Heck, what would I say?

As we turned off the highway toward FM6 and Pecan, bile rose in my throat when the water tower came into view.

We passed the familiar pecan trees lining downtown and then eased down the lazy rolling grass landscape toward the Williams ranch.

I was stuck now.

No way Haley was going in by herself … or maybe nothing would happen.

Maybe it was just my imagination.

Maybe.

Susan and Edgar Williams lived in a modest brick house on the other side of the larger Williams' ranch. It had originally been the Williams' boy's father's house, but Susan and Edgar moved in not long after they were married.

And never seemed to leave.

After driving through the iron gates, winding down the magnolia-lined path, a ringing sound came from the dash, and I jumped so hard my head hit the ceiling.

"Geez, are you okay Miss Leslie?" Haley asked, raising her eyebrows.

"Yeah, sorry just was not expecting that," I mumbled, rubbing the top of my head. Maybe I should have taken a cue from my mama and added in some more hairspray to protect my noggin.

Sophia rolled her eyes, pressing a button on the steering wheel. "Hey Jake, whatcha need?"

"So-so. I thought you were just running a quick errand. What are the kids and I supposed to do for lunch?"

She shrugged, rolling her eyes, though her husband couldn't see it through the speakers. "I don't know. Make them something from the fridge?"

He mumbled something to screaming kids in the background just as Sophia pulled the car up to a parking spot in front of the small craftsmen style house. I could imagine it was probably grand and pretty at one time with its white stucco exterior and big cedar planks lining the porch.

But unlike the other William's grand estate, this one needed a few good coats of paint and someone to take care of the grass and weeds taking over the front lawn.

Glancing back to my friend in the driver's seat, I saw her frown deepening.

Sophia and Jake bickered back and forth as Haley made eye contact with me and mouthed, "I should go'."

"Hold on, I'm coming with you," I whispered, giving a thumbs up to Sophia. "Be right back."

Reaching into the backseat, I grabbed Sophia's bright pink purse, slinging it over my shoulder as I followed Haley up the brick-lined sidewalk.

Sophia stayed in the driver's seat, animated as she gestured to her husband on the phone. Too bad they weren't zooming so he could see all her hand signals.

I wished there were some way I could give her a sign, but it was already too late, and if my pounding heart were as loud as it was in my ears, I was already about to give enough away.

"Hopefully this will be really quick and she'll just ask me the same question she does over and over and then we can leave," Haley muttered as we approached the large wooden door. I guessed the original paint had been a bright red, cheery color; over the years it had faded to a sad mauve. Even the old welcome mat look faded and the porch swing just swung a little bit more crooked than it used to.

"The same question?" I asked.

She nodded. "Yeah, I think she thinks somehow, I can change things with how my dad's trust was written or, you know, that Amber can. I've told her over a million times I can't, so maybe now that you're here, she'll either drop it or really ask you to do her hair."

Swallowing down the breath caught in my throat, I gripped onto the purse straps while Haley rang the doorbell.

Susan opened, the smile slightly faltering on her glossy lips as she adjusted her glasses, looking from Haley to me and then back to Haley.

"Why, Haley, I didn't know you were gonna bring company. Thought it might be just us."

Haley shrugged. "You said you wanted your

roots fixed so I thought bringing a hairdresser might help."

Susan put one hand on her hip and leaned her head back. "Oh, Hales, we both know that wasn't what I wanted to talk about, but since y'all are here, come on in. Is Sophia coming too? Should I get out some sweet tea?"

My feet felt like they were stuck to the walkway as I followed the ladies into the tiny foyer, barely big enough to fit the three of us, the linoleum peeling under our shoes.

While the other Williams family had their large, Texas chic lodge, this Williams family kept it more understated.

And without changing a thing since the former Williams family lived there.

We followed Susan past dark green wallpaper lining the front entry walls to a dark wood-paneled living room, completing the mid-century nostalgia vibe with a sofa and leather recliner that I was pretty sure had to belong to Mr. Williams senior.

"So…. Are we doing your hair or are you going to ask me the same old questions again?" Haley asked bluntly, leaning against one of the built-in bookshelves.

"Oh, don't you worry about me. I'm sure Mrs.

Bev can fit me in another time," Susan said, fluffing her hair.

"Yeah...I thought you went to Mrs. Bev the other day? Isn't that what you said when you came by the ranch?" I asked, using all of the strength I had to get the words off my tongue.

Susan blinked, swallowing hard before she nodded. "Oh, yes, I meant I tried to go there but couldn't get in. You know, since she closes early for Bunco. But it was such a blur that crazy day."

Susan moved her hands like a bird in flight. "I'll be right back. Let me get you all that sweet tea."

She disappeared around the corner into what I assumed was the kitchen, since unlike the newer Williams place, this wasn't an open concept and every doorway lead somewhere new.

Somewhere to hide.

I went to follow her, but stopped when I glanced at the display of photos on the mantel.

Older photos of the Williams family on the ranch, but prominently displayed was another black and white photo I didn't recognize. A man in uniform. Probably from the 1940s, if not sooner.

I turned toward the pictures, my hand tightly gripped on my purse as I looked over them.

"Oh, that's my Paw Paw's photo," Susan said

somewhere behind me, and I froze, my feet rooted in place.

Haley somehow had appeared next to me. "He was a cop? I didn't know granddaddy was a cop."

"Oh, no, honey that's my grandfather. Not yours. Your family were the ranchers."

That's when I spotted the familiar gun in his holster with the wooden handle.

Same one found in the bushes in front of Billy's house.

Just about the time the realization clicked in my head, so did the resounding cock of a gun behind me.

Haley glanced at me out of the corner of her eye, and we both turned slowly to see Susan, eyes narrowed, hands wrapped around the handle of a newer Smith and Wesson.

"Aunt Susan," Haley whispered, her voice trembling, to the rhythm of my own buckling knees.

"Don't 'Aunt Susan' me right now. That might work with your uncle and your late daddy, but you can cut the bull crap with me."

My hands shook as I tried to rack my brain for a way to escape. If only I would have taken those self-defense courses, I'd told myself I'd sign up for.

"Mrs. Susan…what…what do you think you're

doing?" I asked with as much courage as I could muster.

She huffed. "Don't play dumb with me, Leslie. You're way smarter than your ex-husband made you look."

Ouch. No call for that kind of talk.

"Aunt Susan...you should put that gun down. Let's talk about this."

Susan shook her head, her fading red curls bouncing on her shoulders. She may have been short and round, but there was a presence about her in that shoulder-padded blazer. Didn't hurt she was aiming a gun at us either. "I've tried to talk to you and your father, but neither of you will listen, will you?"

"Now let's just talk about this, Mrs. Susan," I said slowly.

"What's there to talk about? Just like when I saw my brother-in-law in that hot tub. He said we could just talk, but that's all we've been doing is talking. But would he give up that land? Nope. Shirley Webster got seventy-thousand-dollars an acre for her daddy's farm in Gunter. We could be multi-millionaires, and Billy didn't give a darn."

She rolled her eyes. "Said he had everything he wanted and wasn't going to sell. Wouldn't do nothing about changing that dang trust passed down from his parents, neither."

"So, you shot Mr. Williams?" I managed to croak.

She blew a raspberry, adjusting her grip on the gun. "That one I didn't mean to. Thought I'd just scare him with my Paw Paw's old gun. I didn't think it would go off like it did. That thing wasn't supposed to be loaded."

She turned the gun toward me. "But this one for sure as heck is."

"Whoa, whoa. You don't need to do this Mrs. Susan," I said quickly, trying to keep the stars out of my eyes as my legs wobbled.

"No, I wouldn't have had to if you would have just quit snooping around. Even cutting your friends tires and rattling up your shop didn't do a darn thing to stop you."

"That was you?" I managed to gasp.

"Geez, you really aren't that bright, are you?" Her smile turned wicked as she took a step closer, the barrel of the gun staring right at me.

"Uh...." I fumbled again for the right words.

This couldn't be it.

This couldn't be my last moments.

"You can't get away with this, Aunt Susan,"

Haley snapped, momentarily taking Susan's eyes off of me so I could grip harder on my purse handle.

"Oh, honey, you don't think I already have? All signs point to you and your little lover doing the crime, so who is that smarmy Dallas detective going to believe when he finds you two dead in here, and I run out crying to the town gossip conveniently outside and tell her that I fought Haley for the gun? Such a tragedy"

The front doorbell rang, the sound clanging off the wood-paneled walls.

Susan glanced back for a second and that was all I needed to grab the taser out of my giant purse and bring it up to Susan's neck.

The electric jolt shot out as I managed to keep it steady. Mrs. Susan dropped to the ground, the gun clattering next to her as she flopped like a fish.

I bent down quickly, my fingers fumbling against the tile as, even in her flailing glory, Susan tried to beat me for the gun.

Out of the corner of my eye, a dash of brown slipped past me, my little Bandit running now with the gun handle hanging out of his mouth.

"Bandit," I cried, not sure if I was happy or frightened to hear the pitter-patter of his little paws.

We'd had a talk about him dashing away with

things, but this wasn't a crawdad. For the first time I was happy to see him sprinting away with his latest treasure.

"This is Detective Adam Waltz with the Dallas PD," a voice boomed behind me.

The back, sliding glass doors now wide open with the detective aiming his gun at Susan and then me.

"Detective, thank god you're here. They were trying to kill me," Susan cried, clutching her hand to her chest.

"What?" I belted, my breath coming out in short waves as I scrambled to my knees.

Adam shook his head as a couple of local cops bounded in after him. One helped Susan to her feet and another two went off down the hallway.

"Susan Williams, you're under the arrest for the murder of Edgar Williams," Detective Adam said, his hard stare locked on her narrowing eyes.

"Wha…what…what? You can't believe it was me? Did you see this woman with the taser?" she spat as the other officer handcuffed her.

"My taser! Glad it was used for something," Sophia piped up.

"I thought I told you to wait in the car," Adam

grumbled, only taking his eyes off Susan once her handcuffs were secure.

"And miss all the fun? Pft. If I was the one to call you, I should at least get some credit."

"You called him?" I asked slowly as Haley helped me to my feet.

"Well, yeah. Once I heard about Mrs. Bev and that whole hair care thing, I started putting some things together. So, after I got off the phone with Jake, I sent a text to Detective Waltz here, telling him he may want to check it out."

She puffed out her chest. "Not gonna say too much, but I'd call me a hero."

Before I could respond, another officer came around the corner, holding Bandit in one hand and a plastic bag with the gun in the other.

"If we're talking heroes, may want to add this little guy too," the officer said, handing me my little brown ball of fur.

I buried my face in his neck, trying to hold back the guttural sob shoved in my throat. "Thank you."

"I'm glad you're okay, Leslie." Adam's voice was softer now as he approached.

Haley and Sophia were talking to another officer writing things down on a note pad, but every few seconds they glanced in my direction.

"Thanks to you and Bandit," I whispered, trying to hold back the shaking in my voice.

"Maybe I shouldn't have been so hard on you. You might have a detective brain after all. Ever think about joining the force?"

I snorted, shaking my head. This was definitely enough excitement to last me for a while. "I think I'll stick with just being the local dog groomer."

He ran his fingers through his hair, now in desperate need of a good brushing. "Well, in that case, since this is getting all wrapped up, and I won't see you around the station. Maybe you can let me and Bandit take you out sometime? There's a dog park and restaurant downtown Dallas…"

I blinked looking up at the sheepish grin crossing his face. "Detective, are you asking me on a date?"

"Um…well…" His cheeks-tinged red. "Just asking if you'd want to meet up sometime. No pressure."

I laughed, for what felt like the first time all day, and it felt good, too. Finally, our little town could get back to normal.

And maybe a new normal was in store.

"I'd like that, Detective."

ACKNOWLEDGMENTS

Picture it, Texas, 2020.

A young author woman is wondering where to go next on her author journey as she devours cozy mystery after cozy mystery. Then, a beautiful young publisher with a love of animals asks if she'd like to submit an animal-themed cozy mystery set in Texas.

That young woman was me and that beautiful young publisher was Molly Fitz.

Of course, then I had to finish writing the book, which couldn't have been done without the wisdom of Emie Lynn with all things cozy.

My Dallas detective neighbors, Kat and Rick, for helping me with police procedurals.

Natalie and her dad for helping me with old fashioned guns and sorry about the whole 'hey-that-old-gun-is-loaded-and-you-had-it-at-your-stomach-when-you-facetimed-me' but it really did help the story!

Classic Pam, for being my guru in all things true crime and the inspiration of course for Sophia.

My own little furballs, Izzy and Breezy, for helping with all things dog. Even when you catch crawdads in the back yard and try to kiss me.

Finally, to my husband and daughters, thank you for supporting me on this crazy journey. I love you all to the other world and back.

MORE BOOKS LIKE THIS

Welcome to Whiskered Mysteries, where each and every one of our charming cozies comes with a furry sidekick... or several! Around here, you'll find we're all about crafting the ultimate reading experience. Whether that means laugh-out-loud antics, jaw-dropping magical exploits, or whimsical journeys through small seaside towns, you decide.

So go on and settle into your favorite comfy chair and grab one of our *paw*some cozy mysteries to kick off your next great reading adventure!

Visit our website to browse our books and meet our authors, to jump into our discussion group, or to join our newsletter. See you there!

www.WhiskeredMysteries.com

ABOUT THE AUTHOR

M. Alfano is a crazy dog lady from a small town in Texas. When not writing cozy mysteries you can find her as the substitute elementary school music teacher or writing contemporary romance under Magan Vernon.

WHISKMYS (WĬSK′MƏS)

DEFINITION : a state of fiction-induced euphoria that commonly occurs in those who read books published by the small press, Whiskered Mysteries.

USAGE: Every day is Whiskmys when you have great books to read!

LEARN MORE AT
WWW.WHISKMYS.COM

Made in the USA
Monee, IL
02 March 2022

92119991R00134